A CHRISTMAS WISH

LYNDA THROSBY

A Christmas Wish
A Novella
Copyright© Lynda Throsby 2019 All Rights Reserved

Editing by Claire Allmendinger of BNWEditing

Cover photograph by Peter Throsby & Stuart Reardon
Cover Featuring – Stuart Reardon & Georgia Conlan
Cover design by Sybil @ PopKitty
Formatted by Cassy Roop @ PinkInk Design

ISBN 978-1-9993150-5-4
Lynda Throsby Publishing
E-Mail ljtpublishing@gmail.com
www.lyndathrosby.com

DEDICATION

To all my family and friends.

Thank you for the support and encouragement you have given me.

To all my readers.

Thank you for taking the chance on me.

Much love
Linda
xx

CHAPTER ONE

Merrigan

ONLY TWO MORE DAYS left in paradise, and the trepidation is starting to set in. I've been cocooned here in the Maldives for the last three weeks. I'm trying to stay as long as I can, in truth, to stay away from home. Home, ha, it's not a home I crave to be in. It's so sterile and pristine everywhere. It's not a normal house that people live in — I mean actually live. You can't make a mess at my home; if you do the maids are there, cleaning it up. Everything has to be in its place. Which is why I'm rebellious, and I leave my stuff all over the place.

I'm dreading going back. It's nearly Christmas, and the wedding arrangements are in full swing. *My wedding arrangements.* The ones I'm not involved in. I just have to turn up. My mother, Queen Astrid Elaine Thornton of Lyntona, yes, that makes me Princess Merrigan Louise Thornton of Lyntona, *sigh*, well, she's had a team working on everything for this wedding. The wedding I don't want.

The Crown Prince of Petura, Prince Carsten Robert Heathcote Suttman, is okay, but I don't have any feelings for him. Both our parents have had this marriage arranged since we were young. I've been friends with Carsten since we were toddlers — our parents getting us together from such a young age, ready for our future together — when I reached twenty-five, which I do the day before Christmas Eve. I don't have a choice with this marriage. We're destined to be together for the monarchy of both our countries.

I live in Lyntona, which is a small European country with a population of about six hundred thousand and it's growing all the time. We have so much beautiful land, which I hate seeing destroyed by more buildings going up. Our climate is very mixed, we have beautiful, hot summers, but we have harsh, cold winters. Carsten comes from a larger country called Petura. It's about a seventy-minute flight from Lyntona and our parents want us to marry to join the countries together, creating a much larger sovereignty. I, on the other hand, prefer our lovely small country and would like it to remain independent.

I'm sitting here on my veranda looking out at the aqua Indian Ocean. It truly is paradise with its beautiful marine life, lush palm trees, and all-round sunshine, yet I know I take it for granted. I know I sound spoilt. We have our own personal island with maids and servants, none of it my doing. I would much rather be here alone. I'm independent. I learnt how to cook from the chef in the palace and have been self-sufficient for a few years now, much to mother's annoyance. She would prefer my handmaid, Cassandra do everything for me. I'm sure mother would have Cassandra wipe my arse if I let her. I love my parents, don't get me wrong, and my younger brother, Archie, but I want to be free. I know it will never happen, and it's my fate to marry Carsten and have his children. I just wish it wasn't, and there was some other way. Some way of passing the crown down to Archie, but he's only seventeen. Mother says he is far too young, reckless, and immature to even consider giving him any kind of power. I tend to agree. But it's mother's fault he's the way he is. She's mollycoddled him right from the get-go. Between her and the nannies, he didn't stand a chance; now he's a real spoilt brat. If he even sniffled, she was there with a handkerchief against his nose and taking his temperature. I know sons in the monarchy are usually what kings want, but the decree in our sovereignty is for the firstborn to be heir to the throne, regardless of gender.

I sip my pina colada and eye the ocean. I love the tranquillity of it here. I tell all the staff not to disturb me when I'm on the island, just stock up the kitchen so I can get what I want, when I want it, and just be myself and be free. I usually bring my best friend's along with me: Jackie, Karen, and Susan, but I wanted to be alone on this trip. It's the last trip before my wedding. My last freedom if you can call it that. Really, have I ever been free? I suppose not.

The wedding is going to be a lavish event with royalty from all over the world attending, along with presidents, prime ministers, diplomats, ministers, dukes, duchesses, ladies and gentlemen. I insisted my best friends were my bridesmaids; it was the only thing I asked for. My mother has picked the dresses for us all, along with the colour scheme, the theme… in fact, everything. I just wasn't interested. I told her over and over I didn't want to marry Carsten, but she and my father would not hear of it. It was a done deal, and no more was to be said about it.

I take another sip of my drink and carry on reading. I look up when I hear a motor and watch as a small boat approaches the jetty to my island. I'm not expecting anyone, so I stand to see who it is, curious because I instructed all the staff that didn't live on the island to leave and come back once I had left, giving them time off. I watch as several people jump from the boat. It's the girls. I squeal and head down with my cover-up flowing behind me, and my hat trying to escape from my head. I hear them all approach the door just as I get there. I fling it open, and we all squeal and hug each other. There's Jackie, Karen, Susan, Julie, Sue, Wendy, Kelly, Jaq, Nastassja and Felicity. "What are you all doing here?" I ask excitedly.

"Well, you, my love, are getting married in a couple of weeks, and we thought where better to have a bachelorette party than here on your island in the Maldives? Not only can we all get filthy drunk and not have to worry about getting home, but we can top up our tans, so we'll look nice and brown in our god-awful dresses the Queen has picked out for us. Have you actually seen the dresses, Merry?"

I shake my head, no at Jackie. "I don't even know the colour, never mind the style." I shrug at them. Jackie rolls her eyes at me.

Karen pushes Jackie to the side to stand in front of me with her hands on her hips. "Merry, they are green, well, jade actually, which was great back in the nineties, but they are great big puffballs. Have you seen that programme, 'Gypsy Wedding'?" I shake my head, no. "Well, they have nothing on us. We look like nineties throwbacks in them. How on earth do any of us pull in those things? Let alone it's being televised all over the world! We will look hideous and be the laughing stock." Karen pouts. She is so dramatic, and the more outspoken, fashion-conscious one out of us all. I laugh at her.

The rest of the girls have gone to find rooms. They all have a favourite room, so I leave them to it and head to the kitchen. I call Bernice to come over and cook for us while they are here. The girls come from affluent families, and none of them are short of money. Some are trust fund brats — well that's how the media has labelled them. We all met at finishing school — the place our parents sent us to learn to be ladies. What a laugh, if only they knew what we actually got up to at school. Of course, it was different for me, as I'd already had a private education. Growing up as a royal, a standard part of my education was being taught how to be a lady, but my mother thought it would be good to send me to finishing school as well. I'm so glad she did. I spent a year in Switzerland and had the most amazing time. I met Antoine in Switzerland. He was my first love, and I lost my virginity to him. It killed me when we both had to go home. We promised to stay in touch, but it faded over time, and I recently saw he had a new girlfriend on Facebook. I do use social media, much to mother's annoyance, but I tell her we have to stay ahead of the game. Everything I post has to be vetted first to make sure everything is politically correct, and I don't post any pictures the royals don't want the public to see. I usually just put a couple of selfies on there when I'm with the girls, and the girls know they aren't allowed to post anything about me.

I arrange for dinner to be cooked for us all — we will eat al fresco. I need to find out how long the girls are staying to make sure I have enough provisions in for them. I was leaving in two days, but I don't mind staying a little while longer. It's not like I have any engagements to attend before my nuptials. Mother left my calendar clear for the months of December and January. To be honest, the longer I stay here, the better, as far as I'm concerned.

I head down to the beach and wait there for the girls to join me. I decide to go for a swim, the sea is aqua-green here on the atoll, and just slightly further out is a reef where I snorkel and watch the sea turtles feed, it's my favourite thing to do. There are a lot of sharks out here, but they are more scared of me than I am of them. I've got used to them over the years. They're only reef sharks so not a danger to anyone. I love it here: the calmness of it, the constant sunshine in the right season, and the smells of the island. It's all so soothing and relaxing.

I'm out in the ocean when I see a few of the girls approach. I wave to them, and they start heading into the sea towards me, disrobing along the way to just their tiny string bikinis and barely-their swimsuits. I'm not the biggest of the group, but I have a good curvy shape, and I'm proud of it. I already have an amazing tan with being here for three weeks. I have long brown hair and a pale complexion in comparison to my father, who is quite dark looking. He is part-Arabic. Apparently, my great, great, great grandmother was an Arabian princess who married my great, great, great grandfather on my father's side. I take after my mother more, although she has fair hair and a pale complexion. Archie takes after my father. He's very broody looking, handsome and he knows it. At seventeen, he certainly has his pick of admiring girls. I know for a fact he lost his virginity at fourteen. I was out in the grounds walking around when I saw him on top of one of the young maids. She saw me and pushed him off her. She was older than him and was very embarrassed. Archie just turned and winked at me with a smirk on his face, the arse that he is, so proud of himself.

After our swim, we all sit around the pool, sipping cocktails and chatting. "Merry, I saw Carsten two nights ago." I look at Susan, wondering why she's telling me this. I raise an eyebrow for her to carry on. "He was out to dinner, but he wasn't alone." Okay, nothing unusual with that. He's usually with friends. He's moved to Lyntona now until after the wedding, then we are expected to go and live in Petura even though I don't want to move from my home island.

"That's nothing unusual, Susan." She looks at me sheepishly. "Come on, what is it?"

She's just about to speak when Julie pipes in, "Oh for heaven's sake, Susan, spit it out. Don't keep Merry waiting." I look at her, a bit perplexed. "He was with Davina Smork. They were having dinner together, and they looked very cosy. They were in the private room at the back of Damska's restaurant. In the room you usually use. Anyway, I was on my phone and went out back near the room as it was quieter to speak there. The door was slightly ajar as I passed, and I saw them in there. The thing was, he was in there eating, but it wasn't his food he was eating." She blushes as she tells me.

"How do you know it was him then?" I ask her. I know he's a womaniser, but I haven't caught him cheating. It would be classed as cheating. Right? Even though we are not actual boyfriend and girlfriend, we are betrothed to be married very soon. He can't be out with other women if he's marrying the Princess of Lyntona.

"Well, Davina had her head thrown back, her mouth open licking her lips, and she was chanting, 'Carsten, that's it, just there, that's the spot, Carsten,' and grabbing the blond head of hair that I could see in front of her." She's bright red telling me this and not by the sun. I can't believe this.

"Tell her the rest, Susan." Julie prompts her, nudging her arm.

"She screamed out with her release. I could see her grabbing his hair and pulling his head tight into her as she screamed, then he pulled away and stood up. He took a napkin from the table to wipe his face." She stops then looks across at Julie, who nods for her to finish. She looks me straight in the eye. "He then said, 'There's no way I'm not getting any of this, once I marry that stuck up princess Merrigan. She better taste as sweet as you do, or I'm moving you to Petura to have you on tap.'"

Oh my god! "Did he say that, the pretentious fucking arsehole?" Yes, princesses swear as well when mad enough.

I'm seething. I knew he had a reputation, but that's cheating. If anyone else had seen him, I would be the laughing stock of Lyntona. I need to speak to mother. I can't marry him. Not now. I'm heading back to the beach to go into the sea again to calm down when I hear a seaplane approach — so much for my solitary peace and quiet. Don't get me wrong, I love that the girls are here but now what? I watch as the girls giggle, and I eye them all suspiciously. We're in the ocean, watching the plane circle. I can't make out who is on it. We watch as it lands and taxis to the jetty, then several people disembark. I squint, trying to make out who it is. There are some strapping males getting out and jumping onto the jetty. The girls are now all primping themselves, straightening out their hair, attire and making sure to plump up their breasts. I see six males heading down the jetty, and I have no idea who they are.

"Surprise," Wendy shouts.

I look at her and furrow my brow. "Who are they?" I ask.

"Well, we couldn't give you a bachelorette party without some hunky, ripped, muscled males now, could we?"

Oh lord, what have they done? My mother will go crazy. "No, no, NO. We can't have anyone else here, Wendy. My mother will go mad. Have they been security checked? Have they signed NDA's? Have they had cell phones removed and searched for any other devices? I need my security."

I head up to the house as quickly as I can before the men get to the beach. I ring for my security and tell them they need to come asap and check these guys out before I allow them onto the premises. I can't chance disgracing my parents with images beings plastered all over social media and the tabloids.

CHAPTER TWO

Devs

I'VE BEEN LIVING ON THE STREETS of New York now for about two years or so, but to be honest, I could be wrong — time means nothing when you're out here. The only thing you know is day and night. You have no idea what day of the week it is or the date — it's inconsequential. I don't 'like' living on the streets, yet at the same time, I find peace in the solitude of it all. Just moving around from place to place, no one to worry about or worry about me. No money problems. Not having to answer to anyone or have anyone answer to me. I don't have any responsibilities. I'm responsible for my survival alone, that's it, nothing else and no one else. In the Secret Ops, I was responsible for my team. They all relied on me to keep them safe, keep them alive, and lead them. I failed.

Don't get me wrong; it's hell not knowing where you'll sleep without any bother, or when and where you'll next eat. There are places to go, and I do use them sometimes, like the soup kitchens, when I'm desperate, which happens often, especially during the winter months. The bitter winter we are having at the moment is a bit of a killer. I've already come across two dead bodies in the old derelict building in Harlem where I've bagged myself a corner. I wonder south of the park daily to find my meals. That's where the tourists are, and the amount of food that gets thrown out there is unreal. The fights I've gotten into over scraps out of a dumpster down a back alley is too many to count. It's a good thing I can look after myself. Being Special Forces, no one stands a chance going up against me. I trained for years. This is a lot easier for me than most, but that doesn't make it easy by a long shot.

However, this is my choice.

I advanced to commander a few years ago, and I led my team from mission to mission. We were one of the most successful teams, which is why we were sent on so many ops. My team was usually sent in to rescue American hostages from the Far East. We were Black Ops, unknown to anyone like the SAS but more secret and more lethal.

My last mission was a failure. I lost five of my men. There were eleven of us, including me. I was responsible for them all. It wasn't the IED that almost killed me. It was losing five of my colleagues and best buddies. Knowing I'd failed them and their families.

We were one big family. We used to get together for family gatherings each time we were home, taking it in turns to host. Most of my men had wives and kids, although there were three of us who were single and liked to play around. I don't think I ever wanted to settle down. I could never stay in one place for long enough. Maybe it was losing my parents at an early age and growing up with my aunts and uncles? I was passed around between them, so maybe I was a handful, who knows? Maybe they just took it in turns, so it wasn't just one of them that had complete responsibility of the burden I must have been.

I vaguely remember being put on a plane when I lost my parents, but I couldn't tell you where from. I don't remember much about them dying. I was just told it was an accident, and I wouldn't see them again. I lived with my Aunt Jasmine and Uncle Tom for the first few years in Montana. Aunt Jasmine was my Ma's older sister. I think it got too much for her to look after me, the more kids she had, so she passed me to my Aunt Jenna and Uncle Mike in Oklahoma. They had two kids, my cousins Dirk and Cane who I have always been close to. Aunt Jenna was my Ma's younger sister. Her and Mike split up, so they passed me to my Aunt Becky in Kansas, she was my pop's sister, and she was single, although she had two kids who were younger than me. I stayed with her then until I enrolled into the military.

I think moving around from each of my family members to different states and then in the military is why I've never settled. I'm grateful for my family. If it weren't for them, I would have been put into the system and who knows where I would have ended up? I excelled in the military, working my way up the ranks. My final rank was commander. We were so successful in our missions. We've rescued sixty-seven diplomats and civilians that had been captured and held as hostages, mainly for the release of their own people being held for terrorism charges. The rest of the world has no idea the magnitude of US captures in the Far East, and that's just the ones, I know of. I know other countries like the UK are in the same predicament as us. All the missions are kept quiet, as are all the foiled terrorist attacks. It's something we were never allowed to talk about.

Our last mission was an ambush. It was a setup. They wanted to capture us and use us against our country. They were going to go public, but it all went pear-shaped. We walked right into their trap. They didn't mean to kill any of us because they wanted us alive to use us as collateral, but their IED went off as we passed. The IED was only small and meant to injure, but they obviously didn't realise there was a landmine not far from the IED, which then ignited and took out five of my team. Three of us were severely injured, including myself, and the other three had superficial wounds. Jacob lost an arm, and Stan lost a leg. I ended up with shrapnel in my torso and a piece in my eye, rendering me partially blind. It's heightened my other senses, which has helped me survive out here for so long.

The weather's turned really bitter. It's late afternoon, and I haven't been able to get any food. It seems I've been beaten to it either by the dumper trucks getting in early because of the bad weather or by the other vagrants who have probably gotten the same idea as me. I need a bed in a shelter for the night if possible because it's getting so cold and starting to snow. I know it will be a fight if I don't get there quickly. I either try for the bed, or I try to eat at a soup kitchen, it's one or the other. I can't have both because the few shelters that do provide food will be full. I decide on the bed. I'll get food tomorrow. I'll get out early and find some food before the dumper trucks.

As I expected, the lines outside each shelter are bad. It's hard finding a bed for the night, but I'm lucky and get the last one in the last shelter I visit. I bunker down for the night, trying to ignore all the noises. This is not one of the better shelters, but it's better than nothing. It's in an old church in Harlem. There are no pews in the church, just rickety old camp beds all lined up in rows. It reminds me a little of being in the military. I'm not new to this sharing, and I have to be on my guard at all times. There have been a few occasions since being on the streets that I have had people trying to pinch my backpack. It holds everything I own, and I would be lost without it. Tonight it seems, is no different. I had just drifted off to sleep when I felt a tug on my pack. I have it secured to my body by the straps and have my arm over it. Are they totally dumb, these idiots? I lift my arm that's across my eyes off my face, and I look at a young guy standing right in front of me. He can't be much older than eighteen. He just looks me straight in the eye, still tugging on my bag. Maybe he thinks I'm an old guy, and he can do what he wants.

"Leave it, son, if you know what's good for you," I say nice and calmly. He cocks his head to the side. He has long, dirty hair that hasn't seen a comb or had a wash for quite a while. His face is filthy, as are his clothes. I know it's hard living on the streets, but at least I'm clean every day. I find a bathroom, and I wash myself down. I get toothpaste and soap from The Samaritans once a month, and I make it last. This is how I have to live my life. Having nice things and being around people is very difficult for me. It's the guilt of it all. How can I have a nice life when five of my men lost theirs? This is my choice.

He's weighing me up. Should he try to snatch it and make a run for it or just leave it? I wait to see what his choice is. If he's smart, he will be thinking it through logically. I would be thinking about how I had to wait for this bed and was lucky to get it instead of being out in the bitter cold and snow. Would I want to lose my bed for the night to risk a backpack that I don't know what it contains? Would I want to risk the guy being able to stop me from taking the backpack and maybe get a beating? Would I be able to snatch it without him getting to me? Is it worth it? I know I would want the bed more than the trouble.

I notice his eyes drift to my chest. He's clocked the dog tags, and he lets go of the straps. He's still looking at me, then he turns and walks away. Wise choice, son, wise choice. No one will get this bag from me, and if he had pursued it, then I would have knocked him out with just one blow. No one would have seen the blow. I'm still agile, even with the injuries I sustained. I manage to get off to sleep without any more incidents.

CHAPTER THREE

Merrigan

WELL, WHAT A DISASTER. Security came and vetted all the guys. They took their ID's, checked them all out, made them sign NDA's, then took their phones from them and made sure they didn't have any other devices on them.

Or so we thought.

With everything checked out, they joined us on the beach yesterday, frolicking with the girls in the ocean, and then we all hung out around the pool, merrily drinking cocktails. I had dinner made for all of us and made sure we had enough drinks to last us. Apparently, the guys were staying for two nights. It's a long way to come for just two nights, but who am I to judge what they do? The girls certainly had a great time with them — well, the single ones anyway.

It's nine p.m. on the second day. The cocktails have been flowing all day, and we're all very merry. The guys have all disappeared into the house, but we stay around the pool. Julie suddenly jumps up, telling us all to follow her. We head into the house and to the large living area. As we enter, I see the guys all standing there, lined up in front of us in full Naval Officer uniforms. I notice the room has been re-arranged. The large couches have been moved to the sides of the room, the tables have all been taken out, and there is one solitary chair in the middle in front of them. I turn to look at the girls, who are all smiling and very giddy.

Oh no. I put my head into my hands. I'm suddenly being moved, by the girls, to the solitary chair. I'm unceremoniously plonked down onto it, and as they scatter to the sides onto the couches, the lights go off, and the music starts. The girls start to holler and scream as I recognise the song from the Magic Mike film. Lights suddenly come on, and the guys start towards me, dancing provocatively. I try to move from the chair, but one of the guys holds me down by the shoulders, while the others start to strip in front of me. I squeeze my eyes shut, wanting this all to end. I'm going to kill the girls for this.

The next thing I know I have Stud, yeah, that's his name, in front of me, in a skimpy Armani thong. He straddles my legs and starts to gyrate on my lap and into my chest. I had no idea they were even strippers. Stupid me, I just presumed they were all friends of the girls. I'm still in my bikini and cover-up as we've been on the beach all day and none of us got changed. He's getting so close, touching me, and I feel really uncomfortable. I start to push him away with my hands on his chest, but he grabs my wrists to stop me. Then he takes one of my hands and places it right there over his very big, stuck out cock. He squeezes my hand, which in turn makes me squeeze his cock, all the while gyrating and thrusting right into me. Is this really what strippers do?

I'm so far out of my comfort zone, even with the cocktails I've been drinking all day. The girls are all hollering and enjoying the performance. I wish I could say the same thing. I turn to face Julie, and I scowl at her, letting her know I am not happy. Stud sits on my lap, and Joey and Bull come to my side, and start to gyrate into me, so I have three of them all grinding around me. I feel the chair start to tilt backwards because Jug, who is behind me, is lowering me backwards to the floor. The other three lift me of the floor, and Jug pulls the chair away. Jug, who is standing above me at my head then falls forward right over my body with his head at my private parts, not quite touching me, and his cock right in my face, which is touching me.

I start to buck my body, trying to get him off me, but in doing so, his nose is right in my private parts, and I freeze. He nuzzles me, smelling, and I'm mortified. I daren't open my mouth to yell at him to get off me, with his cock in my face. He lifts himself off me, and does some fancy dance move and joins the others. I take this as my opportunity to get up. I see the guys all in Armani thongs, gyrating and dancing, moving towards the girls who are all screaming, and I see Nastassja grabbing hold of Todd's thong, pulling him right into her. I'm on my knees, watching it play out as she rips his thong off. He's there, naked in front of her, and I can't make out what she's doing with her hand from this angle, but I see it moving. I then see Wendy do the same thing with Stud, and oh my goodness, what is going on here. This is getting way out of hand, and if I'm not careful, it will turn into an orgy. I start to get up but feel hands on my shoulders. I look up, and Jug is smiling down at me as he dances behind me. I hang my head down, not wanting to see him or watch what's going on.

One of my favourite songs comes on from the Magic Mike movie; Pony by Ginuwine — one of the hottest parts of the film. The girls scream, which makes me look up at them. The guys have them up off their seats, and they are gyrating all around them, provocatively. Just then, I feel my beach cover-up being slid down my arms and untied from around my waist. I try to stop Jug from doing it, but he doesn't let me. The cover-up falls to the floor. I'm on my knees, in just my skimpy string bikini. He comes around in front of me, as I try to get up, but he's holding the top of my head as he dances around me. He stops right in front of me, thrusting his enormous cock that's inches from my face. I close my eyes, not wanting to see, but then hear a rip and automatically look. He's ripped his thong off and is now stark naked in front of me, and, OH MY GOD, his cock is huge.

I'm frozen to the spot, as he's dancing around me. One minute he's on his knees, the next he's on his feet, touching me in different areas, making me squirm, but tingle all at the same time. He drops to his knees again in front of me, and he slowly lowers me backwards, pushing my shoulders. He climbs on top of me and starts the gyrating again, only this time, his very naked cock is right at my core, as he's edged between my legs. What is he going to do? I feel his hand at my hip — he's trying to undo the tie on the bikini. Oh, my goodness, I need to stop this now, once and for all, before it goes too far. He surely wouldn't try to enter me, would he? I slam my hand over his, stopping him undoing my bikini bottoms. He lifts himself over me, and I lift my knee and knee him right in the balls. I see the look of horror on his face when he falls to the side, grasping himself.

I get up quickly, grabbing my cover-up, and I start for the door. I turn the lights on full, then head to the docking station and grab the phone, which has been playing the music into the room. "Get out of my fucking house now!" I scream at them all. I mean all of them, the girls included. I'm disgusted they would let this happen. I'm all for a laugh, but I'm a princess. I'm heir to the throne. I cannot be part of this behaviour. Everyone stops and looks at me. Some of them naked, including Nastassja and Wendy — I'm sure they would be going at it if I hadn't have stopped it.

"Hey, Merry, what did you do that for? We're having a bit of fun. Aren't you enjoying yourself?"

I glare at her. Is she for real, right now? "Are you for real, Wendy? If I had let that go on any longer, I'm sure I would have been raped."

She rolls her eyes. "So fucking dramatic as usual, Merry," she says. "No one would have been raped. It's all for fun. It's your last fling before you marry that fucking pompous, cheating prick. Have some fun, Merry, because lord knows, it will be the last time you do."

I'm seething — my blood is boiling. Is this what they all think? "Get out of my fucking house, NOW, all of you. Go and stay in the guesthouse. Then I want you all gone first thing in the morning."

I storm out and head to my room, locking the door. A short time later, there is a light rap on the door. I open it, and the girls are all stood there, looking sheepish. "What do you want?" I snap at them.

"Look, Merry, we're all sorry it got a little out of hand," Susan says, nudging Wendy as she does.

"Yeah, Merry, sorry for what I said earlier. I was just annoyed because I was enjoying myself. I shouldn't have said those things."

I turn my back on them and sit on my bed. They all come into my room, but I don't speak.

"Merry, look, it was wrong of us. We just thought we would give you some fun before you marry Carsten. We didn't know it would get out of hand like that. We were told when we booked them that they were the best and very professional." Susan is trying to explain.

I hold up my hand. "Look, girls, thank you, I get you were trying to give me one last fling at fun, but those guys went too far. They were trying to undress me, for goodness sake. They were gyrating in my face and nuzzling my private parts. That is not my idea of fun." I'm scowling at them all. "Now if you don't mind, I would like to get some sleep. I want those guys off my island before I wake in the morning. You need to arrange the boat to come and pick them up at first light."

They all look a little forlorn. "Do you want us to leave, Merry?" Kelly asks me. I shake my head, no, before I turn my back on them. They all leave one by one.

I wake up at the sound of the boat arriving to take the guys away, to the airport on Male, I hope. I'm glad they're gone. Now I can just enjoy some girl time. There's a knock on my door and Jackie comes in. "Hey, Merry, I just wanted to let you know the guys have left."

I sit up in bed. "Thanks, Jackie. I heard the boat arrive. I know you all meant well, but that was not my idea of fun. I know I'm restricted because of who I am, but even if I weren't heir to the throne, I would not have enjoyed that."

Susan, Sue and Jaq come in, and they all pile onto my bed.

Felicity arrives with a tray of tea and some toast for us all. We sit chatting for a while. I call for a boat to pick us up and most of us go off to snorkel beyond the atoll where we find manta rays, and on a reef, an abundance of feeding sea turtles.

Back on the island, we're all enjoying the afternoon sun, making sure our tans will be good for the dreaded wedding when I get a call from my mother, which I find strange, especially as this is a facetime call. She normally just leaves me alone when I'm here. I head inside so the girls don't hear my conversation. "Hey Mom, is everything okay? I smile at her, seeing her beautiful face on my screen, only she looks annoyed. In fact, she looks angry.

"What have you done, Merrigan? Have you been on social media today or seen any of the news? You need to get back home now. We have so much damage control to do, and if Carsten calls off the wedding because of what you've done, then I shall have no choice but to renounce you from the throne."

I'm confused, and I must look it.

"Merrigan, what have you got to say? Don't just stand there gawking like a child. What did you do? Is it true, or is this some kind of hoax and damn good editing?"

I have no idea what she's talking about. "Mother, I don't have a clue what you are referring to?"

"I suggest you hang up and search on the Internet for: 'Princess has one last fling'. Then pack your bags and get on the jet at Male airport that will be waiting for you to bring you home. In the meantime, we will try and do some damage control from our side for you. Merrigan, for the first time in your life, I am utterly ashamed of you and what you've done. You have brought shame to our family, to the monarchy, and to Lyntona." She ends the call.

I stand, just looking at the blank screen on my phone as if she was still there. I feel tears running down my cheeks. "Merry, hey, are you okay. Hey, what's happened? Who was that on the phone?" I'm still staring at my phone as Jackie approaches me. "Merry, come here, what's wrong? What's happened? Tell me. You're freaking me out here." She pulls me into her arms, taking my phone from me and hugs me. I sob into her shoulder. I feel like a disgrace, and I have no idea what I have done to upset my mother.

Jackie sits us down on the lounger in the hallway where I was standing. I sniff and then look at her. "Where's my phone?" I'm abrupt, which startles her a little as she passes me my phone. I frantically unlock the screen and do what my mother told me to. There are lots of references to my last fling. I can see some still images of me from last night, in my bikini, sitting on a chair. I click on the top news article from the Mail Online, a British newspaper:

'Princess Merrigan has one last raunchy fling before her nuptials to Prince Carsten'

The Princess Royal, heir to the throne of Lyntona, has today shocked the world with a leaked video of her frolicking with several men. As yet, there is no statement from the royal household. We, at the news desk, received the video from the person who shot it, who can be seen in the video as one of the participants frolicking with the Princess Royal.

Please watch with caution, as the footage is sexually explicit.

There is a link just below, so I click on it and, I can't believe what is playing out in front of me. Jackie and I are just staring at the screen. Whoever took the video placed the device so that it shot everything that happened to me last night, with the strippers. It has been cleverly edited so you don't see me protest or try to get away. You just see what the culprit intended you to see, which was to make it look like I was enjoying myself, surrounded by these guys. There is my voice telling them more, what fun it was, carry on, all of which I never said last night, but they have obviously taken it from speeches I have done in the past. It's very cleverly edited. I'm so mad that I throw my phone across the room. I get up and pace.

"How fucking dare they do this to me. Who shot the video? The guys had their phones removed from them, and they were searched. How the hell did they do this? Or…" I turn to Jackie. "Was it one you lot?"

Jackie jumps up and comes and stands in front of me. "Merry, how can you even think that? We would never do that to you. Never."

I know she's right. I do, but I'm hurt and suspicious. I want answers. The other girls have all come in, and Sue has her phone in her hand, she's pale. She's got the video playing on it. "Merry, I'm so sorry. It's all my fault. This is all on me."

She's crying, and I automatically think it's her that's done this. I get right up into her face. "Explain, Sue," I snap at her. She looks at me with tears streaming down her face. "It was my idea to bring the guys here. I was the one that found them and paid for them. It's all my fault. Please forgive me. I would never do anything to harm you in any way." I'm angry with her, but also relieved it wasn't her who leaked the video.

I turn to go in search of Peter, my head of security. I want to know how one of them had a recording device, and how the hell it got past security.

CHAPTER FOUR

Deus

I WAKE WITH A START. These fucking nightmares — it's the same every fucking night. I sit upright, trying to remember where I am before I remember the bad weather and the old church. I have an old watch in my bag, so I reach for it to see what time it is. It's the only thing I have from my earlier days. My men gave it to me as a thank you for leading them safely on so many missions. It kills me because I let them down, and it also means the world to me. The nightmares are the same, recurring ones. I re-live that day over and over. I see it as my punishment for failing them all. It's kind of like a religious self-flagellation. I can't control it, but I take it as my penance.

It's 5.07 a.m., and I'm sweating even though it's freezing in here. I lay back down, thinking about my nightmares. Thinking of that day and as always, trying to think if there was anything I could have done differently, anything I may have missed. I blame myself for it all, no matter how many people told me it was not my fault. They were my men, my team, and I was responsible for them all.

I lay awake for what feels like ages. I may as well make an early start, try to get some food down me today and see what the weather is like out there. I get my stuff together and go to use the bathrooms that they have here. I don't care about stripping down and having a thorough wash, you get one whenever you have the chance to, but I'm grateful that when I walk into the large bathroom, they have some showerheads on the wall. At least I can keep an eye on my bag in here.

I leave and head back south towards Midtown, where most of the restaurants are. It's a bit of a trek from Harlem, but I won't go through the park, as there is not much food to be found in there. I'm going to head towards 5th Avenue. There's one restaurant there called Casper's. The owner, who is a real hardball of a guy is really kind to me. He caught me one day and instead of just yelling for me to scarper, he actually brought me out some food and gave me bread and fruit to take away with me. Since then, I have been back quite a few times, and he or his wife comes out to give me food if they see me. I've spoken to her a few times; she wanted to know my story. I told her some of it, but not all. When she found out I was in the military, she wanted to help me even more, but I refused. I refuse to let anyone help me. I don't deserve it or any kindness. The food, I will take. I need it to survive out here.

I've had some bits of thrown out food on my way. I need more and to try and stock up. It's bitter out here, and there is more snow on the ground than there was last night. I chose New York because of the population here. So many tourists, which means an abundance of hotels and restaurants, which means so much food being thrown out, but then there are also more homeless here than I first anticipated. Once here though, you kind of get stuck. I could try to hitchhike to somewhere with a warmer climate like LA, but who will give a homeless guy a lift these days? Everyone is so cautious. They don't trust anyone. Shit, I don't trust anyone.

I'm just around the corner from Casper's, making my way there, when I find a dumpster. I'm searching through when I suddenly get hauled out of the way and thrown to the ground. "What the fuck!" I shout. I turn, and there is a big guy, bigger than me, and that's saying something because I'm six foot four. He takes his head out of the dumpster to look at me, and he glares at me. Fuck him. I get up and head back to the dumpster. He moves to block me and faces me. He has long brown hair that hasn't had a wash for a very long time. His clothes are filthy and torn, and he's just in a t-shirt and sweat pants. "Move out of the way. I was here first." I give him a friendly warning. I've had so many fights over dumpsters. The rule should be: first one there gets what there is, but on the streets, there are no rules.

He starts for me. I see his fists balled up, ready to throw my way. He goes to punch me in the face, but I see it and duck my head to the side so he misses, and this makes him go off balance slightly. I grab his outstretched arm and twist it. With one tug, I could break it, but I don't want to do that to him. I don't want him to be hindered even more because living on the streets, is hard enough. I have his arm locked, and he's bent forward because of the angle. "Are you going to leave and not make trouble?" I say to him.

"Fuck you," he spits out. I apply more pressure to his arm. He screams out with the pain.

"Look, man, I don't want to break it. You might not survive out here with a broken arm, so I will ask you again. Are you going to leave and go peacefully?"

"Argh, yes, yes, let me go, you bastard, and I'll leave, argh." I release his arm, and just as I do, he turns and comes at me again. This time, I high-kick him in the chest before he reaches me, and he goes flying backwards, landing on his ass. "Leave now, before I really hurt you, asshole."

He gets up slowly and nods his head. Good, he knows when he's beaten. I watch as he saunters off, looking for another dumpster, before I resume checking this one out.

I only get some vegetable peelings and some gooey stuff that looks like some sort of dessert, but I don't really want that — the sweet stuff can give me the dumps. I head around the corner to Casper's dumpster. I'm having a rummage when the owner's wife comes out. I forget what her name is. "Hey, Deus, it's cold for you to be out here. Isn't there a shelter you can go and stay at to get out of this bitter cold?"

I turn and acknowledge her. "No Ma'am, not really, not during the day. If you're lucky and get there early enough, there are those to stay overnight at."

I start to rummage again. She walks back into the restaurant without saying anything. I find some good bits in here and pack them into my bag. I hear the door go again and she comes out, carrying a bowl. "Here, eat this, it will at least warm you up." She hands me a plastic container with some soup in it and some bread rolls. I sit on the ground next to the dumpster on some cardboard, and I eat it all up, fast. It's delicious, and it's warmed me up. I look up at her, still standing there. She has her arms wrapped around herself, trying to get warm.

"Thank you for that. I really appreciate how kind you are."

"It's our pleasure, Deus. You're a military man. You served our country. Now let us serve you."

I look at her face, and she's smiling. The door opens again, and Casp comes out and stands with her. He reaches out his hand to shake mine. "Hi, Deus, nice to see you again. I see Macen has been looking after you." He smiles at her, and I see the look they give each other. My heart melts slightly at the love they clearly have for each other. He has his hand around his back, then brings it forward and holds out a bag to me. "Here, these are a few bits for you. I know you are a proud man, but Macen here insisted. Please don't be offended." I take the bag from him, and I pull out a pair of thermal gloves and about six pairs of thermal socks. I have on fingerless gloves, it helps when rummaging for scraps, but I take these. They will help when I'm not rummaging.

"It's for the winter months, Deus. I can't bear to think of you out in this cold, freezing your toes and fingers off. Please accept them. It's just a small gesture." She looks slightly embarrassed.

"Thank you Ma'am, Casp, that is very kind of you both. I really appreciate it, and they will help me a lot."

The smile on Macen's face is priceless. She looks like she wants to jump up and down. "I would do more if I thought you would let us, Deus," Macen says. I get up from the floor. Casp holds his hand out to help me, and I take it. Not many people would come near a homeless man and touch him, never mind help him. These are good people.

"Thank you, both, but what you do is more than enough for me." I salute them and walk off. They make me feel good for a moment but then, I wonder what would they think if they knew I killed five of my men. They wouldn't want anything to do with me.

I flit around more dumpsters and get enough food in my bag now for today and tomorrow. I make my way to one of the nicer shelters to see if I can get a bed for the night. It's so bitter, and it's snowed nearly all day. I take off my old fingerless gloves, which are very thin with holes in now, and I hand them to a homeless woman I pass. Might as well see if someone else can use them. I put on my new gloves. They are a blessing in this cold.

I have to walk to three shelters before I find one with a spare bed. This one also serves soup, so I at least get something warm inside me again. I settle for the night, and the nightmares I know will come.

CHAPTER FIVE

Merrigan

WE'RE WAITING FOR THE boat to come and collect us, bags packed. I've been sifting through the Internet — the video is everywhere. It's gone viral. I feel so ashamed of myself. I'm to blame. Peter said all the guys were searched thoroughly, and they all complied with the search. The only thing he can think of is that one of them hid a phone or camera somewhere when they got off the boat before security checked them. This makes sense. They planned this before they even got here. I look up. "Sue, did they know who they were coming to surprise? Did you at any point mention my name to them or the island they were going to visit?" She sits, pondering my questions and shakes her head, no. I carry on looking at all the articles. I'm torturing myself, I know it, but I want to see. On my social media, there is so much support for me being 'normal', but then there is also a lot who say what a slut I am, and I should show some respect to my family that I'm a disgrace and should be thrown out of my country. I also have guys messaging me; being so vulgar it makes me sick.

I react when my phone is snatched out of my hand. "Hey, I was reading that."

"That is the problem, Merry. It's going to do you no good reading anything that is being said. You're going to go stir crazy."

Ha, I already am. I scowl at her and put on my best authoritative voice. "Karen, pass me the phone." She glares at me and shakes her head, no. "I said, pass. Me. The. Fucking. Phone. Now, Karen. I'm telling you as your monarch, not at your friend."

She has no choice than to pass it back to me. I get up and head to the kitchen, ignoring them all. I feel them all staring at me as I go. Well, fuck them. It's their fault my life has gone to shit.

I sit in the kitchen on my own, but I don't go back on the Internet. I'm staring at the black screen of my phone when it rings. Ugh, my mother. I slide to answer, but I don't speak.

"Merrigan, are you there, Merrigan?"

"Yes, Mother."

"It's not good, Merrigan. The video has gone something they call viral. They say there is nothing they can do about removing it."

I already know this. I know once something is on the Internet that's it, it's out there, and there is nothing anyone can do about it. "Huh huh."

She takes in a sharp breath. I know my mother, and that's a tell-tale of how angry she is. "Is that it? Is that all you have to say?"

"What do you want me to say, Mother? I don't think there's any point in trying to say anything anymore."

She sighs again. "Has Carsten been in touch?"

He did ring me a couple of times, but I just ignored him. He's the last one I want to speak to right now, especially after what Susan told me she'd witnessed. "No, Mother."

She sighs again. "I see I'm not going to get anything from you. When will you be home? The jet should be there already. Where are you now?"

"Still on the Island waiting for the boat to arrive."

"I will see you when you get back. I have to say, Merrigan, your lack of concern at this moment for the shame you've brought to your father and I, and the monarchy, leaves a lot to be desired, young lady. Your father and I want to see you the minute you arrive back. Have Felix take your cases to your room and find us immediately. Do you hear me, Merrigan? We have an awful lot to discuss about your future in this family." She hangs up. She doesn't even give me a chance to answer her or to even say goodbye. She hates me, and she's disgusted with me, I can hear it in her tone. They're going to renounce me, which to be honest, is what I want because then I don't have to marry Carsten. But now, maybe he doesn't want to marry me anyway, so being renounced isn't quite so appealing.

I rest my head on my arms on the kitchen island surface, and I cry. I cry that my mother and my father now hate me and are ashamed of me, and this was not my doing. I don't want to go home only for them to tell me they want me to leave again. I don't want to face them, although this has sealed it for me that I'm not marrying Carsten. I don't like him, and he's a philandering, cheating cad. If he's doing this now, before we marry, then what will he be like once we are married? We're marrying out of duty, not love. He will get it anywhere he can, and I can't have him disgracing the monarchy once we are married. I certainly don't want to have children with him — that thought now repulses me.

I can't do it. I can't face any of them after what's happened, and I'm not marrying Carsten.

My phone rings, and I lift my head. Talk of the devil, and he shall appear. I answer in silence. "Merry, Merry, are you there. Merry talk to me."

"I'm here," I say curtly to him.

"Why are you being rude to me when you've disgraced us all and made such a fool of me?" I snigger at that one. "Merry, I find your attitude very disturbing. You have disgraced us all. Did you sleep with them?"

"What?" I scream into the phone.

"I said, did you sleep with them? I need to know, Merry. Are they going to show videos of you in an orgy with them? I need to know what happened so I can prepare myself when the press asks me about our marriage."

What a nerve he has. "You have the nerve to ask me if I slept with them after what you've been seen doing in in the back of Damska's with Davina Smork, you arsehole. Don't you dare question me! Are we not engaged to be married? That would mean being faithful to each other regardless of us not loving each other. I've been faithful, have you?" He doesn't speak "What, cat got your tongue now, hey, stud?" I put the phone down on him before he can speak. I'm so angry and hurt right now.

The phone rings again, and I ignore it. It rings and rings and every time I hit reject until eventually, I answer. "What do you want, Carsten?"

He sighs. "I don't know what you've been told, but it's all lies. It wasn't me!"

I laugh aloud. Is he serious right now? "Oh, I'm sorry. My source must be mistaken. There must be another Prince Carsten that Davina knows because that was the name she was shouting out as she was being eaten under the table and screaming while you were giving her an orgasm."

I hang up on him again, put my phone on silent and put it in my pocket. I don't answer when he rings back. I've had enough of everyone. They are all judging me, and I'm so angry with the girls. I wish they had never decided to come and visit me. Why couldn't everyone just leave me alone?

I hear the boat approach and the girls moving to get their bags. I slowly lift off the stool and make my way to the door. I grab my Louis Vuitton bag and head to the jetty. I don't speak to anyone, and they are all quiet the whole journey to Male. In the airport, I make a rash decision. I tell Peter my security to leave me alone, and that I want to go to the bathroom without him tailing me. He protests as it's more than his life is worth to leave me, but I make it very clear he will not be my head of security if he doesn't go to the private lounge and wait for me there.

I head to the reservations desk and book myself on a flight to Atlanta. I don't want to go home. I don't want to see anyone, especially not Carsten, and I can't bear the look of disappointment on my parents' faces. They're going to make me leave anyway. I may as well make it easier for them all. I'm not even going to tell the girls.

My new flight is scheduled to leave before the jet. I tell Jackie I want to be alone. That I don't want to speak to anyone right now, and that I will see them on the jet. I tell Peter to stay put, that I'm fine. He gets up to follow me, but I tell him I will fire him. I stay in the main area of the airport on my own. That way, he can still see me when he pops out, which I know he does. All I have with me is my handbag and my passport. I don't have any clothes.

I have my credit cards and a little bit of cash, but that won't last long. As soon as I see Peter go back into the lounge, I get up and find the currency exchange counter, and I get a few thousand US dollars on my credit card. Getting them here is safer than in the US. My mother will trace my cards. She will soon know I've gone to Atlanta because I had to use my credit card to buy my ticket, but I plan to get the train from Atlanta to New York if I can, using the cash. That way she won't know where I am. I then nip into the souvenir shop, and I buy a long beach dress and a big floppy sun hat. I sit back where I was, fully aware Peter has seen me shopping, but as long as he can see me, he won't be concerned with what I am doing.

I keep an eye on the departures board. Male is only a small airport, so I need to be careful when I leave to board my plane, making sure none of the girls are around, and Peter doesn't spot me boarding a different flight. This is going to be so hard. I'm sitting near the boarding gate so I can see when everyone has boarded. That way, if I'm last on board, once he realises I'm not around, it won't matter. He will run around the airport looking for me, but by that time, I'm praying the plane will have taxied off to the runway. When I see nearly everyone has boarded, I turn and see Peter. I mouth to let him know I'm going to the bathroom and shoo him back into the lounge with my hand gesture.

I rush to the bathroom, put on my new long dress, untie my long hair so its all loose and falls over my face, put on my floppy hat and sunglasses, then I cautiously make my way to the gate to board, hoping no one recognises me, and that Peter hasn't noticed it's me in new clothes. I hurry through passport control, where I get a funny look. I just shrug and put my finger to my lip in a hush, and then I rush out onto the tarmac to climb the stairs to the plane. I'm holding my breath and my hat as I do, expecting to hear Peter's voice with every step I take, but it doesn't come. I don't turn around as I reach the top of the stairs. I get into the plane as quickly as I can. I'm the last on board. I settle into my seat in economy, yes, I chose economy so I didn't bring any attention to myself. I wait for the doors to close, on pins expecting Peter to appear at any moment. The captain tells the stewards to close the doors and prepare to take off, and I have tears rolling down my face. I've done it. I've got away. I know Peter will be frantic, and I also know he will face the wrath of my parents, and he may lose his job. For that, I'm really sorry. Maybe one day I can make it up to him.

I have an old man next to me, trying to start talking to me, but I just want to be alone. I put my ear pods in, pretending to listen to music, but I don't want to waste the battery on my phone, so I don't actually listen to anything. I do manage to sleep for a while. We have a stop off at Dubai on the way, then I board another plane to Atlanta. I'm sure with the stopover it's about twenty-four hours in total before I to get to Atlanta. Great.

I like Dubai airport, especially the Emirates terminal. There is everything you could possibly want; it's huge. I've never actually walked through it before. With being royalty, you are whisked away from the airports. I never get to see any of them. I grab something to eat, then I get a few bits of clothes and some essential toiletries. I'll get some more when I get to the US. I have no idea what I'm going to do and exactly where I'm going to go, and I'm starting to worry about my decision already. I switch my phone on, and it blows up with hundreds of missed calls and messages from all the girls, my mother, Carsten, even my father and brother.

I decide to listen to a few messages. Some are from the girls, frantically telling the kidnappers to let me go and not to harm me if they listen to the message. Oh no, I didn't think this through.

I don't want to put my phone on when I land in the US, as I know my mother will have put a trace or some kind of tracker on it — it's protocol for royalty. I text my mother to say I'm fine and will be in touch when I'm ready, but I will not be marrying Carsten… that will go down well. I then text Jackie and tell her I'm fine and to let the rest of the girls know I haven't been kidnapped. She replies straight away, asking how she can know this isn't the kidnappers texting her trying to throw her off the scent? I text her back telling her who she lost her virginity to, as we are the only two that know that it was my brother. She's happy it's me and tells me stay safe and keep in touch.

I switch my phone off, ready to board my flight to Atlanta.

CHAPTER SIX

Merrigan

SEVENTEEN HOURS IN ECONOMY on a crowded plane. I have never flown economy until today. Not fun — not in my eyes anyway. We are just disembarking and my goodness, it's freezing. I forgot it's December, with being in the Maldives and it being so hot there, I didn't even think about how cold it would be here. I only have a beach dress on. I get one of the t-shirts that I bought in Dubai out of my bag and put that on, but I need more. As soon as I get to some shops, I'll be buying jeans, sweatshirts, boots and a thick coat.

I'm just about to go through immigration, and I'm on pins in case my mother has contacted the authorities to look for me. I wouldn't put it past her. I also have a royal passport. I hope they don't think it's a false one and interrogate me. Royalty would not be going through immigration this way. I would not normally have to clear immigration on my passport. Royalty can travel almost anywhere our country has a treaty with.

I approach the desk and hand over my passport. The immigration officer scans it, then he looks at it quizzically before eyeing me suspiciously. Oh shit. Has it alerted them on the system? It's probably flashing up red. "Your Highness, Ma'am, shouldn't you be entering the country through the dignitaries area? Why are you clearing immigration?" Oh shit. I look at him quite sternly so he doesn't think I'm a pushover. "My jet had a fault, so I booked myself onto a normal flight to get to Atlanta to visit with my friends. Please, sir, can I kindly ask you don't make a scene, as I would hate for anyone to recognise me and cause problems in the terminal for you. I would just like to go and meet my friends if that is okay with you?" He slightly bows to me. I think I've shocked him by being here. There is no mistaking it's my image on my passport, but to be honest, he would have no idea what Princess Merrigan of Lyntona looked like. He lets me through without saying anything else and without having to have fingerprints or my picture taken.

I know my mother will know where I am as soon as I clear passport control, which is why I will get the train to New York. Using the train doesn't require a passport.

I head out to arrivals, and I find the nearest shop to buy some warm clothes. It's an American Eagle Outfitters store. My teeth are chattering, and I need to cover up well. I buy a backpack to put all my bits in and the clothes I have on. I buy a thick coat with a fur hood, a red woolly beanie hat, red scarf and some fingerless gloves, only because that was all they had left. I can't believe how cold it is, and I haven't even gone outside yet. I'm so tired still from all the travelling. I need a bed, but that will have to wait. I stand

and look around. It's so Christmassy everywhere. There is a huge tree full of baubles and lights in the middle of the arrivals hall, and there are decorations everywhere and Christmas carols being piped through the ceilings. I forgot it was approaching Christmas. There's even a Santa ringing his bell. I pass and put a hundred dollars into his bucket. With the impending wedding and being in the Maldives, Christmas itself completely slipped my mind. I start to feel homesick seeing the tree. My mother has a tree sent to her every year from Queen Sonja of Norway. The staff takes days to decorate it, and it's one of the highlights of our Christmas. I always used to help them decorate it. I'm feeling so nostalgic right now. I feel like getting on a plane and heading straight back home.

I snap myself out of it, remembering why I'm here. I need to find the train station. I get a train to downtown Atlanta, and then I can get an Amtrak train to Manhattan. It takes about twenty hours. I have to leave straight away, as they'll be able to trace me to Atlanta.

Having never done anything like this for myself, I've done pretty well so far. I'm on the train to Manhattan. I paid cash, so there is no trace of me unless they somehow can get all the CCTV footage of me. I settle into my private room on the train. I splashed out for premium to get a private sleeping room, so I could at least have a good rest. I know it's extravagant, but I just needed to be able to sleep properly in a bedroom and take a shower.

Many hours later, I arrive at Penn Station and head out to the streets. I've been to New York a few times with my parents on state visits, but I've never wandered the streets of New York alone, and it's scary. It's snowing and freezing, even with the layers I have on. I sneeze, hoping I'm not starting with a cold. Going from thirty-five-degree temperatures to what feels like minus ten is a shock to my system. I start to walk, but I have no idea where to or in which direction. I need to find a hotel too, but it will need to be a budget hotel. I've spent nearly a thousand dollars already on clothes and the train. I need to make my money last as long as possible because I have no idea how long I'm going to stay. Will I go back home and face everyone there, or move onto somewhere else? The second, right now, is my favourite option; somewhere a lot warmer than here. LA or Vegas would be good. Maybe I should have headed to one of those? I just thought of New York because it's so crowded, and I can get lost here. I can just blend in with everyone else.

I wander around for a while, still not knowing where I am. I think this is an area called Hells Kitchen and I'm starting to feel unsafe. There are so many hotels. I just need to pick one. I go into one that looks clean enough. They have a room, and it's not too expensive. I settle in, then decide to go out and find somewhere to eat. I'm walking around, fascinated with this real world with real people, living real lives. I don't get to see this at all when I travel. I'm chauffeured from one luxurious place to the next. I fly on private jets or take private yachts. I stay in penthouse suites in top hotels. I never see the real world.

I get something to eat in a diner — everything I'm doing is new, and I love this independence I have. I go for a cheeseburger, fries and a strawberry milkshake. My mother would have a fit if she saw me now. I watch all the people passing by as I sit here eating. They all seem to be in a rush, everyone power-walking along, and I sit wondering what their stories are. I like people-watching. I sit for a little while, watching life pass me by outside.

I keep thinking about home. My home. If I go back will I still have a home? Mother said they wanted to discuss my future after the video fiasco, and I took that to mean she would go ahead and renounce me from the throne. That means Archie becomes heir to the throne, but I'm sure it won't be for some time. He needs to grow up first. Being renounced doesn't worry me at all. I never wanted to be Queen in the first place, but I don't want to lose my home.

I decide to head back to the hotel. It's gone dark outside now, freezing cold with snow everywhere, and I need to get warm and have a good night's sleep in a comfy bed. I hope I can remember the way back to the hotel. I just walked and walked until I came across this diner. I head back in the direction I think I came. There are fewer people out now. I'm much more aware of my surroundings, but it all looks so different at night-time. I go down the streets that I think I came along, turn onto one street, and regretting it the minute I do. There are some men just standing around, smoking and talking. I stop in my tracks. There are a lot of run-down houses on this street and lots of rubbish and graffiti. One of the men notices me, and he nudges one of the others until they are all turned, looking my way. I start to turn to head back because I don't remember this street. I must have taken a wrong turn somewhere. How naïve am I? This is typical me, sheltered my whole life, so I don't recognise danger when I see it.

"Hey, pretty lady, stop." I hear one of them say. I walk back the way I came. The next thing I know, he's in front of me, stopping me in my tracks.

"Excuse me, please," I say and try to walk around him. I hear more footsteps approaching. The others are now in front of me. I turn and start walking quickly down the street I wanted to avoid, but they catch up to me, and I feel a tug as one of them grabs hold of my handbag. Shit. I start to panic. He tugs and tugs really hard.

I try to keep hold of it until I feel it leave my shoulder. I look at him, he has a knife in his hand, and he's cut the shoulder strap to take it off me. Shit, everything I have is in that bag: my phone, my money, and my passport. He moves away. "Please give me my bag back."

They all laugh at me. "What kind of a bullshit accent is that?" one of them asks me. I don't speak. "Miss lardy dah, cat got your tongue?" one of the others grabs my arm. "Come on, speak, we want to hear you say something. Where you from with an accent like that. Miss snooty?"

"Please, leave me alone. Can I have my bag, please?" I try to tug out of his grip, but it just tightens. He then grabs my face under my chin, squeezing my cheeks. I'm terrified.

I'm looking him straight in the face. He has a tattoo under his right eye, a teardrop that makes him look sad. He has his nose pierced and his eyebrow. He gets right into my face. "Where are you from, Princess?"

Shit, does he know who I am? They must know me. Why would he call me princess if they didn't know who I was? I start to panic. I try to break free from his grip, but the more I struggle, the tighter he gets. "Where are you from, bitch?"

I can't talk. His grip is so tight. I try to say Lyntona to him. He doesn't understand, so he releases his grip on my face. "Lyntona, I'm from a small European country called Lyntona." I spit out at him. "Never fucking heard of it. You speak like the Queen of fucking England though."

The man who took my bag is rummaging through the internal pockets. "Fucking bingo!" he shouts. He's found my money. I watch his face light up as he registers how much there is there, fanning it all out in the air to show the others. I think there is probably about three thousand dollars, but I'm not sure, it could be more. They all start to holler, and the man who has my arm suddenly kisses me on the lips hard. "Fucking A, you stuck up bitch. Mummy and Daddy must be rolling in it." He tries to imitate my accent, doing a very bad job of it. He grips me tighter, pulling me into his chest.

The other men are counting the money and looking through my purse to see if there is anything in there. They take my credit cards and read my name: "HRH Merrigan A Thornton. What kind of a name is that?" I don't answer. I'm now being squeezed tight, right into the chest of the man who has hold of me. He wraps his arms around me so I can't fight him. His hands wander to my arse, and he squeezes, pulling my tighter into him. I spit in his face, shouting, "Get off of me." He releases me and wipes his face. I try to make a run for it while he's distracted, but he tackles me to the ground, and I go down with a thud, screaming as I hit the pavement hard with my head. It hurts, my vision goes blurry, and I think I blackout for a few minutes.

I come to, on my back and a man is on top of me trying to undo the buttons on my jeans. He manages to get them undone, and I scream, I can't remember what's happened, but I know this isn't right. He tries to cover my mouth, and I manage to sink my teeth into the side of his hand. He punches my face hard, then pushes my head, making it bang really hard on the pavement. I scream again. Where is everyone? Why are there no people around? Where am I? I can't remember, but this is wrong, why would I be in the street with someone on top of me, hurting me.

He tries to put his hand down my jeans, and I buck, trying to get him off me. He's too heavy for me, so I shout and scream again. He's getting closer and closer to my private parts, trying to pull my jeans down as he does. Oh no, how do I get out of this? I scream more, shouting for help. "Shut up, bitch, before I kill you." As I lift my head, he pushes it back down, and I smack on the ground again.

Suddenly, he's gone. One second, he's there on top of me, the next, he disappears. I close my eyes. What's happening to me? Me... who am I? I can't remember my name or why or how I'm here. I hear a lot of noise, and I lift my head very gingerly, whimpering as I do at the pain shooting around inside it. It's all blurry, but I can see what's happening. The man that tried to rape me is laid out on the floor with blood all over his face and his hands in a very peculiar position. I see two other men running away, holding a bag, and then a man is beating another man to a pulp on the pavement. I have no idea who they are and who the other guy is that's doing the beating. I don't know who is the good guy and who is the bad guy. I try to get up. I get to my knees, and just as I try to stand, I go toppling backwards onto the pavement with a thud to my backside. My head hurts. I rub it, and there are a couple of big lumps, one on the side of my head and one huge one on the back. Shit, what happened?

Who is the man beating on the other one? I don't understand what's going on. I rub my face as that's also hurting and it stings. Just then, a shadow comes over me, and I look up into a terrifying but beautiful face. Eyes that are pale brown with eyelashes are so long any woman would be envious of them bore into me. I could get lost in them. Is he going to hurt me? Is he one of the bad men? He leans down, and I try to shuffle backwards away from him. I must look like a startled cat caught in headlights. He stands up straight and holds his hands up to show me he means no harm. How do I know that? He could be a bad man for all I know. He points down at me, and I look at what he's pointing at. My coat is hanging off me, and my top is up, showing my bra. I quickly pull it down and wrap my coat around me. He holds out his hand for me to take. I just stare at him, wondering what to do now.

CHAPTER SEVEN

Devs

I HEARD A WOMAN SCREAMING as I was walking up the street, so I ran to see what was happening. I saw four guys, one was on top of a woman, but she wasn't moving as I approached, then suddenly she started to buck him off, screaming, telling me she didn't want him on top of her. One of the other guys was just watching them, and the other two were crouched down on the floor with a women's purse. I pulled the guy off her and threw him to the floor. At a glance, I could see that her top was up, exposing her chest, and her jeans were undone and looked like they were being pulled down. I pounced on him, grabbing his hands. I bent those fuckers back until they snapped. "Don't ever lay a hand on a woman again unless she asks you to, do you hear me, fucker?" He screamed in pain but nodded his head. I slammed my fist into his nose, breaking that too. I'd knocked him out, and blood was pouring everywhere, turning the white snow crimson around his head.

I got up and grabbed the other guy who was still watching. I don't know if he was on something, but I punched him, and he didn't budge from my blow, which is very unusual, so I took him down and pummelled him. The other two ran off with her purse. I turned to see her try to get up but fall back. I quickly moved to try and help her, but she was terrified of me. I could see the fear in her eyes. I stepped back and held up my hands and pointed at her top so she could cover-up. I held out my hand, offering to help her up. "Hey, it's okay. I'm not gonna hurt you. I just need to make sure you're okay."

She weighed me up, assessing if she could trust me — if I was one of the bad guys or a good guy. I tried to reassure her, softening my face, trying not to look so scary, but that was hard to do after seeing those guys attack her. I waited a few minutes, letting her compose herself and take in her surroundings.

I crouched down in front of her, and I could see she had marks on her face, one side was all scraped, and the other was red and looked like it was starting to swell. She was the most beautiful woman I'd ever laid eyes on. *Not the time, Deus.*

"Hey, my name is Deus. I heard you screaming, so I came to see what was happening. Are you okay? Can you talk? Do we need to get you to a hospital?"

She's looking at me warily. "I don't know," she manages to croak out.

Okay, that doesn't help. "You don't know what? Are you okay?" I decide to ask her one question at a time.

She's thinking. "I think so. I'm in pain. My head is throbbing, and my face and arms hurt." She rubs her arms.

"Do we need to take you the hospital to get checked out?"

"I don't know. I think I will be all right." She has a cute accent. I would say she was English from the sounds of it.

"Can I help you up? You fell back just now trying to get up. Do you feel dizzy or nauseous?"

She nods her head slightly and winces. "I do actually, yes."

I smile to myself a little because she's not answering my actual questions. "Let's try this one question at a time. Can I help you up?" she nods but winces again and goes to grab her head. I can see the pain she's in. I get to my feet, take her hand and hold her elbow to steady her and pull her to her feet. She stumbles a little, but I catch her before she falls backwards. I have hold of her arm, and I tower above her. I look down, and she looks up. Wow, she sends jolts of lightning to my stomach. "Now, next question, do you feel dizzy?"

She nods slightly again. "Yes, I do feel dizzy, and I think I'm going t…" she throws up, just turning to the side in time so she doesn't vomit all over me. Well, that answers that one as well.

"I think it best we take you to be checked out at the hospital. There's one not too far from here. Do you think you can walk there?"

She nods again, grimacing. "Do you mind if I help you there. I don't want you to keel over again. It means I need to put my arm around your waist to stop you falling. Is that okay?"

She looks up at me startled. "I - I guess so." I do just that, and I pick up my backpack that I dropped just before I reached her. I sling it over my shoulder and start to help her to the nearest hospital.

"What's your name?"

She looks up at me, furrowing her brow. "I have no idea. I

don't even know where I am or why I'm here. I think I banged my head, hard. It really hurts here and here, see?"

I look at where she points on her head, and I can see a lump the size of an egg in each place and blood on the back of her head. That's not good, especially if she can't remember anything. She may have a concussion. "Okay, I'm going to call you… hmm, what?" I look around us as we walk, and just then I hear one of Santa's helpers on the corner with his bell. "I'm going to call you Belle."

She looks up quizzically. "Why Belle?"

"Santa was ringing his bell over there." We both laugh, but then she frowns and holds her head as I stop her from falling.

We head into the ER at Mount Sinai West. I don't know if they will see her. She doesn't know her name or anything, so I doubt she will have medical Insurance. I explain at the desk that I found her being attacked, and she has a couple of bad head injuries and some memory loss. They say they will see her but for her to take a seat and wait to be called. I tell them that I call her Belle.

The receptionist looks at me strangely, and it's then I see that she has just realised I'm homeless. "Don't worry, sir, you can leave, and we will take care of her. We will call the police to take a statement from her."

Like hell. I'm not leaving her until I know she's going to be okay.

"No, I will stay with her and make sure she's okay. Besides, the police will want to take a statement from me as I was the one who saved her from being raped and beaten on more."

She nods at me. I return to Belle, and we wait to be called. One thing at least, it's warmer in here than out there. I've been to all the shelters looking for a bed for tonight but got no luck this time.

"Hey, Belle, do you remember anything about yourself at all? Where you live? Where you're staying? Do you live in New York, or are you just visiting?"

She looks at me and shrugs, giving me a sad, confused look. "I don't know Deus. I've been sitting here trying to think. Do I live here, or am I visiting? I honestly don't remember." She puts her hand to where the lump is on the back of her head. "Ouch."

I laugh at her, and she scowls at me. It's then I notice the true colour of her eyes, they are aqua green, and with mousy brown long hair and the most perfectly shaped lips, she is flawless. I'm staring at her, but I can't help it. She scowls again. "Sorry, I erm, well, just you're, you know, oh never mind. Anyway, don't touch your head and it won't hurt. Is your head still throbbing? Do you still feel dizzy or nauseous?" Well, I nearly put my big foot in that one.

"Okay, smart arse. I know it won't hurt if I don't touch, but it's just instinct to want to rub where it hurts. I still feel a little dizzy, not so much nauseous now." She smirks at me. "Well, that's good to know. You almost got me back there, with your projectile vomiting." She laughs then instantly goes to hold her head. "Ouch," she grumbles, scowling at me again as if it's my fault.

Two police officers come into the ER to the desk, and I see the clerk point in our direction. I stand as they approach us. "Good evening, Ma'am, we had a report you've been assaulted. Is that correct?" he asks her, eyeing me up as if it's me that attacked her. He looks me up and down, taking in my threadbare clothes, and I know the minute he clocks I'm homeless because his whole demeanour changes towards me. It's like they have no respect because you're homeless.

"Yes, I was, officer. I don't remember much, I'm afraid. I banged my head and haven't been able to remember anything, not even my name. I know Deus here saved me though."

She looks at me fondly and smiles. I smile back. The officer looks at me again. "What can you tell me, erm, Deus is it?" He heard her. I tell them what happened from the point where I came into it, and I swear they don't believe me. I bet they think it was me that attacked her and because she can't remember, I'm now playing the saviour. Pricks. I wipe my mouth with my hand, and it's then he notices the bruises on my knuckles. Maybe he'll believe me now. They radio for someone to go and check the area to see if the guys are still out cold on the ground. I hope they are. They deserve to freeze to death out there after what they've done to Belle.

They ask her similar questions to me, but she can't tell them anything. There isn't a lot they can go on. She has no ID, and she can't remember anything.

A nurse calls out, "Belle."

She doesn't respond, but I hear it and tell her that's for her. She gets up, and I see her wobble a little, but she stays upright. She disappears with the nurse. The officer gets a call on his radio. I hear them say no one is there, just some blood in the snow. He turns to look at me. "Well, Deus, thank you for helping her, but I think you can leave now. We have your statement. I don't think there is any more we need from you, as there is no one to press charges against you."

Huh, me? "What, press charges against me? What bullshit.

For saving a woman from being raped and beaten. What a fucking crock of shit."

He steps closer to me, taking out his notebook again. "Watch your tone, Deus. What's your full name?"

Fuck now he's going to look into me. "Amadeus Stollinka."

He looks at me with a frown. "That doesn't sound like a very American name. You here illegally?"

I could punch him. "No, I'm a US citizen of no fixed address."

He walks away to radio in and get me checked out. Probably making sure I don't have any priors or outstanding warrants. I sit back down. I'm waiting for Belle regardless of what they say. I want to make sure she's okay.

He steps back to me, but I don't look up when he approaches. "Sir, you can leave now."

Sir? He just called me sir for the first time. I guess that means he has just been told I was a decorated commander in the military. That's the only time anyone shows me respect.

"If it's all the same to you, officer, I will wait to make sure Belle is okay before I leave."

He thinks about it, then nods and walks away. He comes back a few minutes later, and he passes me a coffee and a bag. I take them from him. There is a sandwich and some fruit in the bag. "Thank you, sir. You didn't have to do that."

He shrugs. "I know, but I wanted to. You saved her tonight and hopefully gave those thugs what they deserved. It's just a small gesture."

We chat for a little bit. Him asking me how I came to be homeless and where do I stay. I don't tell him everything, just that I prefer having no responsibilities, and I stay where I can.

I hear my name being called by a nurse. I stand up and head

towards her. "We're keeping Belle in for observations tonight. She asked me to thank you for everything but not to waste your time waiting around for her."

Well, shit, if that isn't telling me to take a hike, I don't know what is.

"Can you tell her I hope she remembers soon and gets to where she should be — where she belongs…" I start to walk back when I hear my name again. I turn, and this time it's Belle.

"I'm sorry. I wanted to say thank you myself. You will never know how grateful I am that you were there to save me. I will forever be in your debt, Deus. I just don't want you wasting your time waiting." She's a little unsteady on her feet. The nurse grabs a wheelchair for her. "Right, Belle, let's get you to a bed for the night. You shouldn't be up on your feet."

"Belle. I'm going to wait if you don't mind me hanging around? It's not like I have anywhere else to be, is it?"

Her whole face lights up, and I see a sparkle in her eyes for the first time. That is until the nurse pipes in, "Sorry, sir, but you will have to leave the hospital. This is not a place for you to keep warm. There are shelters for that."

Well, that's a smack in the face. I see the sad look on Belle's face. She turns her head slightly, giving a pleading look up to the nurse, but the nurse just shakes her head, no.

"Excuse me, Ma'am, if I could just have a word?" the officer interrupts us all. They walk off to the side.

"I'm sorry Deus, I hate the way you're being treated because you're homeless. Some treat the homeless like they are lepers, and it's so wrong," Belle offers.

I shrug just as the officer and nurse return. "Sir, I will take you to the family room where you can wait for your girlfriend.

Unfortunately, this will be all night, as she has to be under our observations for the night. If you follow me, I will show you the way." The nurse grabs the wheelchair and starts wheeling Belle.

I turn to the officer and hold out my hand. "Thank you, sir, for this. I wasn't doing it to stay out of the cold. I want to make sure she's okay."

"I know you do son, I know." With that, he leaves, and I follow the nurse and Belle.

CHAPTER EIGHT

Deus

In the family room, I think back to seeing Belle on the ground with that thug on top of her. I was so outraged and disgusted at what he was doing that I wanted to rip his arms off for touching a woman like that. It's beyond me how anyone can treat a woman like that. I hope she gets her memory back, then at least make sure she gets back to where she belongs.

Being on the streets, you learn to sleep through any noises, and I drop off. I feel someone touch my arm, and I jump up, startling Belle, causing her to jump back. Shit, I nearly knocked her flying. "Belle, I'm so sorry. Hey, are you okay?"

She smiles at me and looks at my hand on her arm. I quickly drop it, and her smile fades. "Actually, it's Merry."

I'm confused. What's Merry? "Huh, Merry Christmas to you too." I laugh at my own joke.

She smiles. "No, that's my name, Deus. Merry. I remembered. They said the rest should slowly come back to me, but at least I know my name. Merry, I like it. It does remind me of Christmas. In fact, now I'm saying it, I think I love Christmas. I'm sure it's my most favourite time of the year."

Wow, Merry. I like it too, but I like Belle better. "Okay, Merry Belle, oh that has a nice ring to it?"

She laughs at me, although still holding her head. "I take it with all the Christmas decorations out there that it's nearly Christmas?"

I smile at her. I like that she doesn't know stuff, and she doesn't wear a ring, so I take it she isn't married or engaged, but it doesn't mean she's not in a relationship. Not that it matters to me. I'm just a homeless guy. She wouldn't want anything to do with me.

"Yes, I think it must be nearly Christmas. Although I'm not sure. Living on the streets, the days all roll into one, and you never know the day or date." I shrug. She places her hand on my arm and looks at me sympathetically. I don't want sympathy. I deserve this life. If only she knew.

"Have they cleared you to leave now?" She nods very gingerly, yes.

"Okay, so what have they said?"

"They said I have a concussion, but the swelling will go down. They took me for a scan, and there is no bleed on the brain from what they could tell, so that's all good. They said not to be alone for at least forty-eight hours just in case." She looks down. She's messing with the hem of her sweatshirt, which is a bit dirty.

"Hey, what's wrong?"

She looks up at me. "Oh, Deus, I don't know where I've come from so how can I not be alone for the next forty-eight hours? I don't have anything apart from the clothes I'm in, and I don't have anywhere to stay." She sits on the chair I was in and puts her head in her hands.

I crouch down in front of her, take her hands away and lift her chin gently. "Merry Belle, I don't have anything to offer you. I'm homeless myself. I live on and off the streets. I find shelters when it's bitterly cold like it is now. If I had a place, I would not hesitate to let you stay there. I'm so sorry, but I can't help you." I wipe my thumb very softly over her grazed cheek. She doesn't flinch or move. In fact, she's stopped breathing. Shit, maybe I shouldn't have done that. I move my hands away and stand up.

She looks up at me, hurt, but at least she's breathing again. "I'm sorry Merry Belle." I grab my backpack and head to the door. I turn back. "Please take care, I hope you get all your memories back, and you find your way home." I see a tear slip out the corner of her eye as she looks at me, all sad and forlorn. Shit, I feel so bad, but what can I do? I can barely look after myself out there, never mind having responsibility for someone else. I can't do that. Not again. I can't be responsible for anyone other than myself.

But I still feel like the biggest shit ever as the doors slide open for me to go out. The bitterness of the cold hits me in the face as I turn to leave. It's no more than I deserve for leaving her, but I can't help her. I'm sure the nurses will help her find somewhere to stay.

As I step onto the sidewalk, I turn as I hear her call my name. She comes running out of the door to me. "Deus, I can't do this. I have no one else. I don't have anywhere to go. I don't even know where I am. I'm scared, Deus, I'm terrified of being out there on my own. I will never survive. I don't have the first idea of where to go for help. What if the men who attacked me come looking for me to finish what they started? You're the only person I know. Oh,

Deus." She throws herself into my chest, hugging me and crying. I hang my head, thinking about this. I'm so ashamed with myself for leaving her. My gut instinct is to help her because well, that's who I am. I'm a protector. I can feel my heart pumping like crazy in my chest because it means spending more time with her, but my head is saying, no, you can't do this. You can't look after anyone else.

I feel her hand on my arm, but I don't look at her. "Deus, hey, Deus, look, I'm sorry. I'll go and ask at the desk and see what they suggest. Hey, Deus, are you okay?" I slowly move my head, nod very slightly, and look her in the eyes. I want to help her so much. I really do, but how can I look after her? She doesn't belong on the streets. I could tell straight away she was more polished than most people I've met. The way she speaks. Her skin flawless, her nails well manicured, her hair long and shiny. She is perfectly groomed and has the manners to go with it. It's just the clothes that put her out of place: a red hat and scarf, fingerless gloves, skinny jeans and a blue parker coat with a fur hood — just normal high street clothes. Maybe she's a student or something, living here?

"I'm sorry, Deus. Thank you for everything you've done for me — for saving me from who knows what. You will never know how much I appreciate it. Look, I will just go inside and ask them. I'll leave you now. I can see you're slightly stressed by my suggestion, and I don't want to cause you any more stress. Are you sure you're okay though? You're sweating and very pale?" I wipe my top lip and my brow on my arm. I'm cold, so I don't get why I'm sweating. She's right, I'm stressing about being responsible for her if I help her. I feel like I'm about to have a panic attack thinking about it. I turn on my heel and walk away, leaving her standing there. I can't do it. I can't do it, I chant in my head, walking away. I start to slow my steps, and then I stop. I'm a coward for leaving her there, for leaving a beautiful woman alone, not knowing where she is or who she is. I'm the lowest of the low but, I can't do it. I just can't. Coward, I shout in my head. I'm going into meltdown. Keep it together, Deus. I feel like a shit. Should I turn and go back? No, I can't do it.

I cross the street, and turn down an alley as though I've disappeared, but double back and stand out of view, but where I can see the hospital entrance. She's not there now, shit. She must have gone inside. I didn't turn as I walked away because I didn't want to see the sad, helpless, lost look on her face.

Walking away killed me. I'm officially the biggest loser and idiot going. I've had plenty of sexual relationships in the past, but never one to settle, they have only ever been short or casual. I have never had feelings for anyone in the way of 'wow I want this person forever' kind of way or had butterflies ever when talking to a woman. But with Belle, it was immediate. She is absolutely stunning, and I had fuzzy feelings when I was near her, but also the Neanderthal in me wanted to come out and just take her in my arms and protect her from the world, especially after the attack she just endured. I would have ripped that fucker's arms off if I could so he couldn't touch another woman again. I'm getting angry thinking about it. My eyes are glued to the hospital entrance, and it's not too long before she appears again.

She is covered up with her coat, luckily as it's bitter out here. I watch as she just stands there outside the hospital, wrapping her arms around her body to try to stay warm. She looks both ways, up and down the street, I guess wondering which way she should go. She's all alone. She has no one and doesn't even know who she is. I can't just leave her. I need to help her. I need to get over my own fears and help her out. What if she gets attacked again? Wandering around the streets of New York on your own is not the safest thing to do. I need to go and be with her and protect her until she gets her memories back at least. Then, once she knows who she is, we can make sure she gets back home safely, even if I just make sure she gets to a female shelter. I know they are still not ideal. I know women attack each other, beat on each other and rape each other in those places. I've heard it all, being out here. Maybe a mixed shelter, that way, I could make sure she stays by my side. That would be better. At least I will know she's safe.

I start to walk over the street, still at war with myself in my head. I stop, then I start again, then I stop. I must look like a crazy person, stopping and starting, tapping my head. She's been standing there for ten minutes, not knowing what to do or which way to go. I approach cautiously, and she doesn't notice me, she's so lost in her thoughts. I'm still telling myself to turn around when she sees me. "Hey," I say sheepishly. "I was still in the area, well, over the street actually. I couldn't leave you to fend for yourself out here all on your own, Merry Belle."

She gives me a great big smile, flies into my arms, hugging me to her. I just manage to catch her. "Whoa, Tinker Belle." She laughs, and it's the best sound I've heard in forever. I smile at her.

"Thank you, Deus. Thank you for coming back for me. I was terrified. I couldn't move from this spot. I didn't know which way to go or what to do. Deus, I'm so scared, but I do remember something else now, my name is Merrigan, and it's Merry for short. I think it's coming back slowly. I don't think it will be long."

I smile at her. She's still in my arms, her face next to my face, so close. I look at her lips and lick my own. She notices and goes red. This is intimate, I want to kiss her so badly, but I can't go there, no matter what I feel. She'll remember who she is and she'll be off to live the rest of her life, as she was before. I slide her down my body to her feet.

"Come on, let's see if we can get some food, and then we need to make our rounds and find a shelter that can take us both in for the night. Because of the bitter cold and all this snow, they'll fill up fast. If we don't get a bed in a shelter, it's back to my place." I smile and wink at her. I've just realised I haven't smiled in forever. I've had nothing to smile about. Merry Belle comes into my life, and all I seem to do is smile. I head to the one place I'm almost guaranteed some food if the bosses are there. It's still quite early, but they should have some scraps before the dumpster truck comes along.

We start walking in the direction of 5th Avenue where Casper's is, and we talk as we walk.

"Deus, why didn't you want to help me back there at the hospital? Yet you've changed your mind now? You looked like you were going to have a meltdown at one point."

She stops me walking with her hand on my arm, and I face her. I take a deep breath. I'm not ready to tell her any of this, so I shrug. "It's hard enough looking after myself, without the responsibility of looking after someone else out here, Merry Belle. I just didn't think I could do it, but then I felt like a shit walking out of that hospital and leaving you. I hung around to see what and where you would go. I was in a war with myself about coming over to you. I don't do responsibility well, Merry Belle."

We're facing each other, and I notice a tear fall from her eye, so I wipe it away with my thumb. She takes in a breath at the touch of my thumb on her face, and she looks me in the eyes and smiles that perfect smile of hers. She melts me with that smile.

She shivers from the cold as we start to walk again. I put my arm around her shoulder and pull her into my side to try and keep her warm. She looks up at me and smiles again. I smile back at her. On 5th Avenue, she looks around in awe. "I love this time of year, Deus. All the Christmas decorations make me so happy. It's my most favourite time. We always had a big tree, and we had people to dec…" She stops and looks at me. It's then I realise she'd just remembered that. "Wow, I remember, Deus. I remember I love Christmas time." She starts twirling in the middle of the sidewalk, and passers-by are looking at her like she's crazy. Admittedly, she does look kind of crazy right now. I know it won't be long until she remembers her life. It's starting to come back gradually now. We continue walking, with her getting giddy about the Christmas windows in the shops and the decorations everywhere.

We approach the back of Casper's, and I head to their dumpster. I turn her to face me, and I crouch slightly so we are at eye level. "Now, please don't get grossed out, but this is what we have to do to survive out here, Merry Belle. We have to search for food in these dumpsters." She looks at the dumpster, then back at me and scrunches up her face. I laugh at her. I know exactly what she's thinking. I was the same the first time I had to do this. I take her hand and show her what kind of stuff we are looking for. She gets right in there with me. She doesn't let it faze her at all. The only thing she complains about is the smell.

"Hey, Deus. I saw you on the screen in the office. I've brought you some soup and bread." I look behind me at Casp, who's holding out two cups of soup and some bread for us both.

"Thank you so much, Casp. I don't mean for you to keep doing this. I'm sorry." I hang my head.

"Hey, nonsense, only too glad to help you and your friend.

Here, take these. I'm sure Macen is getting some stuff together for you both right now."

Just then, Macen comes out the back, holding a brown paper bag out to me. "Hey, I'm Macen, nice to meet you." She holds her hand out to Merry Belle. These two have to be the nicest people I know. Merry Belle introduces herself to Macen, and they start to talk, I hear Merry Belle telling her about her attack and her memory, and how I saved her and am now helping her. She's making me sound like a hero when I am the furthest thing from a hero.

Casp and Macen leave after talking for a while. I grab some cardboard and place it on some stairs to keep us off the snow on the ground and we sit for a little while, eating our soup and bread. I'm sitting behind her, watching her. I feel so protective. We leave Casper's with a bag full from Macen and some other scraps in my bag — enough for both of us today. We head to the shelters to find a place for us both. The first four have nothing but the fifth one has two beds left. Perfect.

We manage to get two beds next to each other. There is no way I'm letting her out of my sight. I even go with her to the bathrooms and wait for her outside, making sure to listen for anything unusual. I make her stand outside while I use the bathroom and ask her to talk to me the whole time. She even starts to sing. She has the smoothest voice, and she starts singing Christmas carols. I'm blown away by her singing. When I come out, I see she has an audience, who love her singing as much as me. She's beaming at me. "I remembered the Christmas carols. I remember singing them in church. I think if we visit a church tomorrow, it might help my memories." I agree. We settle for the night, and I pull her bed right next to mine. I have my backpack at the side of me, and I hold her hand tightly. I wake in the morning still holding her hand, but also tucked under my arm. It's the best feeling ever.

CHAPTER NINE

Merrigan

I WAKE UP TUCKED UNDER Deus's arms, holding me close. I love it, and I love how protective he is. He makes sure I'm safe at all times. There is a lot more to Deus than he's telling me, but I don't push him. He will tell me when he's ready to. I'm so glad my memories are coming back slowly. Maybe it won't be long before I remember everything. I know Christmas is a magical time, but this right here with Deus, and even living like this, is magical. I feel alive. I feel like this is the first time I've lived, and I don't know why. I feel as though my life has been suppressed to this point, and suddenly I've been set free. He kept hold of me all night. I have never felt so protected, or at least, I don't think I have. We use the bathrooms, and he gives me soap and toothpaste so I can get cleaned up, then we head out to find our food for the day.

As we step outside, I go to get my hat and gloves out of my

coat, but they're not there. I run inside, back to my bed and search, but they're not there either. Deus runs after me wondering what's wrong. "Oh, Deus, my hat and gloves are gone. Someone must have taken them. It must have happened during the night, but I didn't feel a thing."

He comes over to me and hands me his gloves and hat to wear. "No, I can't take them from you, Deus, you need them as much as I do."

"Hey, I'm used to being on the streets. I don't think you are, so you need them more than I do. We'll find you some more from somewhere." He pulls me into him and hugs me, rubbing my back.

The snow has melted a little since yesterday, but it's still freezing. He takes me to some more dumpsters for us to get scraps. I feel bad for him that he has double to look for now, with me tagging along, so I get right in there and search with him. The truth is, if he hadn't come back for me, I don't know where I would be right now. Not knowing where I'm from, or what I'm doing is, so frustrating. I wish I could remember. I wish I knew my life. I hope that when I do remember, it's nothing that will take me away from Deus. I hope that I can help him like he's helping me. I know he's struggling with something and he has issues. Maybe I need to make a Christmas wish? Do I believe in them?

We get food for the day, and the snow has started to come down much thicker. We've been to a few shelters but haven't been able to find a bed for us both, and he refuses to leave me alone. "Sorry, Merry Belle, it's gonna have to be back to mine I'm afraid, as long as no one has pinched my corner." He gives me a sad half-smile. I know from the look on his face that this is going to be rough on me. We start walking towards Central Park. "It's over on the north side of the park, in Harlem. It's an old, derelict building, but as long as no one has claimed my corner, I have boxes to help protect me from the cold." He shrugs. "It helps a little."

I link his arm and snuggle into his side as we walk. I'm also aware I have his gloves and hat on, and I feel bad. I'm more aware of my surroundings now, more alert. I look around, and I stop. "Hey, Deus, look at that church over there. It's so beautiful. Can we go inside, please?"

There is the most beautiful church across the street, and when it's clear of traffic, I start to cross the street so I can try and read the sign. "Oh, wow, Deus. St Patrick's Cathedral." I turn to him, smiling and at seeing the joy on my face, he smiles back. "Is it open? Do you think we could go inside? It looks beautiful." Just outside, below the steps on the sidewalk is a Santa Claus. He has a bell and a bucket, collecting money. I read his sign aloud "All donations for A Christmas Wish Foundation go to help children in need." I look up at Deus. "I wish I could help in some way. Those poor children. Everyone deserves a wish to come true at Christmas."

He looks at me, cocking his head to the side. "You just amaze me, Merry Belle. Here you are, homeless, not a penny to your name, freezing to the bone, and you want to help the children in need." He smiles at me, then leans in and kisses the tip of my nose, pulling me into his chest. I'm a little shocked, and I feel the heat rising from my chest to my face at the affection, but I love the comfort of it. Maybe I was starved of affection, and this is all new to me? I don't know. It just feels strange. Or maybe I have someone who loves me, and I feel some guilt because I love being in the arms of this man holding me.

The doors of the cathedral open as people are coming and going. I make my way up the steps, pulling Deus behind me by the hand. I'm dying to see the inside. It looks so serene. As I open the inner doors, I hear the beautiful sounds of a choir singing. "Oh, how amazing is this?" I say to Deus, but when I look at him, he isn't listening to me, but to the choir. There are people sitting in the pews, watching and listening. I can see up at the front there are four, beautifully lit Christmas trees, all adorned with white lights and nothing else. Two of them are on the actual altar, and the other two are on either side, at the bottom of the steps. There is a huge nativity scene to the left of the altar. The stained glass windows shine bright, and the huge organ is high up above the altar.

I sit down and look around in awe at the place. I feel so peaceful in here and safe. I start to sing along to the Christmas carols that the choir are singing. There are people coming and going all around us. Deus is watching me sing along with the choir, as I get lost in my own little world. I close my eyes and sing my heart out. I remember this is something I used to do all the time at our cathedral in our city. The cathedral I grew up to love. I can picture it in my head, very similar to this one in its grandeur. I can picture me sitting up at the front and looking back at the cathedral, full to capacity. I remember doing this almost every Sunday, but it wasn't just me sitting there. I can't quite remember who would sit with me.

My eyes fly open, and I stop singing. "Deus, I remembered someth…" I see the smile on his face, and he nods his head. I look around, and I see there is an audience. I lean into Deus. "Why are all these people watching us?"

He laughs at me. "You have no idea, do you?" I shake my head.

"Merry Belle, your voice is like an angel's, so smooth. You were singing along with the choir, but it was your voice that shone through. You were lost in the moment, which, in turn, got all of us lost in your moment." I blush, not sure what to say. Everyone starts to move away, leaving us, although a few people come to me, and shake my hand, telling me how beautiful I sounded.

After everyone leaves, he gently takes my chin and makes me look at him. He strokes a finger down my cheek to my chin. "Hey, Merry Belle, that was the most amazing thing to listen to and to watch. You have the sweetest voice. It's like you were in a trance while singing. I can't describe the sound. It was just so angelic and mesmerizing, like the sirens of the sea who used to entice the sailors into the ocean, where they would meet their fate."

"Oh, you mean the mermaids." I look at him, and I start to remember. "I remember that. I remember it was my favourite story growing up, and I remember a woman reading it to me a lot. I just can't make out who she is or what she looks like." I tell him what I remembered while I was singing. "Maybe you sang in the choir yourself, where you come from. Maybe that's why you wanted to visit a church today."

Just as we are about to leave, a man of the cloth approaches us. "Ma'am, my name is Monsignor Richard Ruder. I am in charge of this beautiful house of God. I have to say, I heard you singing just now along with our choir, and you sounded so beautiful. Can I ask, do you sing in church normally? You sounded as though you did this often. Your voice fits perfectly with the choir."

Oh my, I'm taken aback at all this attention just from me singing. Maybe it's what I did do before I lost my memory? I explain to the Monsignor what has happened to me and that I don't really know. He's very sympathetic. He asks for us to wait a few minutes, and says that he will be right back. I nod, look at Deus and shrug. We listen to the choir while we wait, and I hum along this time, not wanting to draw attention to us again. It's not long until Monsignor Ruder is heading towards us, handing Deus a bag. Inside are some clothes. "These are from our lost property box. No one has ever been back to reclaim them. Please take them and make use of them. There are some warm clothes in there, which will help you during this cold time. Anytime you want to come back in here and sing, you are more than welcome. In fact…" he stands thinking about something. "What would you say that for the next couple of weeks, at least in the build-up to Christmas, you come back here once or twice a day, both of you, and you sing for us, Merrigan, along with the choir? I will make sure you have food and hot drinks each time you come. We have so many visitors to our beautiful cathedral. I'm sure they would love to hear you sing." I look at Deus. I'm with him wherever that may be.

"What do you want to do, Merry Belle? Would you like to sing each day?"

I don't know. I feel shy and embarrassed. I look from one to the other. "I think I would like to sing, but I'm not sure I can stand in front of an audience to sing. I don't know if I have ever done that before. Deus, what do you think? I'm with you on whatever you decided. I'm already a hindrance and a burden to you. I don't want to put you out any more than you already are. This will interrupt your routine and may stop you from finding a bed in a shelter. I can't let that happen every day. I feel bad enough." I hang my head.

The Monsignor is listening to us. "Please excuse me for interrupting, but I can make sure you both have a bed in a shelter — one that the cathedral supports. It's not the Ritz Carlton or anything like that, but it is one of the nicest shelters there is. If you do decide to sing, Merrigan, each day at least for the next couple of weeks until Christmas, I will guarantee you both hot food and a bed each night. I hope this at least helps take the burden of finding food and shelter away from you both for a short time."

Wow, that sounds amazing, and I would be doing something that I think I love. I look at Deus cautiously. He's not sure about this. I can tell by the look on his face. Maybe he can release me as his burden and carry on as he was, and I'll stay, sing and get shelter. I don't want him doing something he isn't comfortable with.

"Deus, I understand if this is not something you want to do. I know you like to come and go as you please. You're independent, and you're used to finding your own food and shelter. I understand if you want to leave me and do your own thing. I'm not your responsibility. You didn't do this to me. On the othe…"

He puts a finger over my lips to stop me talking so much. "Merry Belle, if you want to do this, I would not stop you. I can tell you feel strongly about the church. It also means you get hot food and a bed. You should do this."

"But what about you, Deus, do I lose you if I choose to do this? I don't want to lose you."

He's thinking about it. He takes my cheeks with his hands and lifts my head. "You won't lose me, Merry Belle. If you choose to do this, then I would be a fool to turn down hot food and a bed, but most of all, knowing you are being looked after and safe. I can't bear you being on the streets because you clearly do not belong there. I'll stay with you for as long as you want me and need me too. You're not a burden to me. You're like an angel sent to me." He leans in and kisses the tip of my nose.

I know I stop breathing when he does this. The Monsignor coughs quietly, reminding us he's still there. Deus drops his hands and looks at the Monsignor. "I think Merry Belle would like to take you up on your offer. I would like to also offer my services in return. If you need anything at all doing, I can sweep up, or I'm a good handyman if you need anything fixing."

The Monsignor bows to Deus, holding his chest, "It would be our pleasure to have you both. I'm sure we can find some odd jobs for you to do, Sir."

Wow, I can't believe this is happening. Hopefully, my memories will start to return more now they are coming back gradually.

We leave the cathedral and head to the shelter that the Monsignor gave us the address for so we can secure our bed for tonight. I promise we will be back for the evening service, and I will sing with the choir but out of view.

CHAPTER TEN

Devs

WALKING WITH MERRY BELLE tucked into my side, I feel so proud of her for some strange reason. I've only known her a couple of days, but she amazes me. There is no way she belongs on the streets. I don't think from her accent that she's from the USA, but I can't place where it's actually from. I don't think she is from money — her clothes look like normal high street clothes, and she hardly has any jewellery on her, just some pearl-like earrings that don't look real, but then what do I know about jewellery? I did notice how tanned she was in the hospital, which means she can't have been in New York for long, as it's been freezing here for weeks. Ah… her watch. I stop us walking and turn her to face me. "Merry Belle, I noticed when I was putting my gloves on you this morning the tan mark on your wrist as though you wear a watch. Do you think you had one on and those thugs who attacked you took it from you?"

She pulls her hand out of her glove and looks at her wrist. "I didn't even notice, Deus. I certainly have a good tan though, looking at how white my wrist is, where I must have worn a watch." She sighs and shrugs. "I couldn't tell you if I had a watch on or not. I can't even tell you why I have a tan. " She closes her eyes. I hate she doesn't know anything. I pull her head into my chest and rub her back to comfort her. She must be so frustrated.

I pull away from her and look into her stunning eyes. "Hey, it will come back to you. It's gradually coming back now. I'm sure it won't be long. The floodgates will suddenly open, and you'll remember everything. You'll remember you're a princess and run off into the sunset back to your life of luxury." I laugh, hoping to God it's nothing like that. She gives me a small smile. "All I'll see is a puff of smoke left behind as you run off back to your life." I laugh trying to make a joke of it but secretly hating the thought.

She doesn't look happy at that, and she slaps my chest hard. "Don't joke about it, Deus. What if the life I had was terrible? What if my memory loss is my way of coping with a shitty life? What if I was in an abusive situation? What if…" I shut her up, putting my finger over her lips and bending down to kiss the tip of her nose.

"Merry Belle, I don't see any tan lines where there would have been a ring, so I take it you're not engaged or married. That doesn't mean you were not in a relationship. You're very tanned, which tells me you've been on holiday because if you lived somewhere that hot, you wouldn't have tan marks like that."

She's staring at me, eyes wide and her head tilted to the side. "How are you so observant, Deus? I hadn't even thought of any of that, and with my education, I certainly am not behind the door if you know what I mean. I …" she stops and puts a gloved hand over her mouth.

I stand, watching the expressions change on her face. She's remembering something, and it's something important. "Deus, I think I might come from an affluent family. I remember being in a room when I was younger and a lady showing me something in a textbook. It looks like schoolwork. I don't know if it's my mother or a teacher? Damn, why can't I remember it all, why is it just fleeting images?"

I take her hands in mine and squeeze. "Why do you think you were wealthy? It could have just been your mother?" She shakes her head, no. "I don't think it was. She was young. I looked about ten years old, but it wasn't just that. The room I was in was stately. I saw paintings of people on the walls behind the lady. There was lots of floral wallpaper and gilded light fixings over the paintings. The ceiling was very high with a picture rail going around the top. I remember all that from that fleeting image. To me, that says wealth?" She's right unless it's an image that's stayed with her from visiting somewhere.

I grab her hand. "Come on, let's get to the shelter and secure our beds, grab some hot food, then chill out before we get you back to the cathedral for your first show.

She laughs. "It's not a show. It's just me singing — something I enjoy doing."

Chill out, where did that come from? I've never chilled out with anyone in my life.

I'm pleasantly surprised when we get to the shelter. I didn't know about this one, and I thought I knew all the shelters in New York. I know the Monsignor said it wasn't the Ritz Carlton, but to me, this might as well be. It's clean and welcoming. The people running it are nuns and volunteers of the church. We secure our beds next to each other, and after eating some soup and bread, we sit facing each other, talking. I'm scared she will remember more, so I try not to question her.

"Deus, do you mind if I ask how did you become homeless?"

Shit, I suppose it's the most obvious question to ask. I'm not going to lie to her though. "I made myself homeless, Merry Belle, I had a bad time and couldn't cope, so I did this. It's my choice."

She looks sad, and it pulls on my heart. "Does it have something to do with you not wanting to be responsible for anyone? You said that to me outside the hospital." I rub my hand over my face. I'm not ready to go there yet. I turn and lay on my bed with my arm behind my head.

"Yes, Merry Belle. I had a job where I was responsible for people, and something happened. After that, I didn't want any responsibilities in my life, so I packed my bag and became homeless. Life has been anything but easy trying to survive on the streets, trying to avoid any type of conflict, but I don't have any responsibilities, so in my eyes, life is good." I turn my head and see her watching me. I smile and pat the side of my sleeper. She smiles back then comes and lies at the side of me. I put my arm around her. "You know, Merry Belle, this is the first time in such a long time I have ever just chilled. I have always been on the go, looking for food all day and then finding somewhere to sleep. I feel quite relaxed for the first time in years." She doesn't speak, and I peek down at her. She's asleep. I pull her into me more and take comfort from her. I don't know what she's doing to me. I've never had feelings like this for anyone.

I feel myself shaking — someone is touching me. I jump up quickly, on my guard, and I startle Merry Belle. She's standing next to my bed. Shit. "S-sorry, Deus. I didn't mean to make you jump. I just wanted to let you know I was going to make my way to the cathedral. I don't want to be late. I didn't want to wake you, but I thought you would panic if you woke up and wasn't around."

I look at her. She looks terrified. I bend over, putting my hands on my knees, letting out my breath. "I'm sorry, Deus." She starts to move away.

"Wait, Merry Belle, look, I'm sorry, okay? You just scared the shit out of me. You're not going alone. I'm coming with you." I grab my backpack, then take her hand and start to walk away, pulling her with me.

She yanks her hand from mine. "Deus, you stay here. I appreciate everything you've done for me, but I don't want to put you out any more than I have. I can get to the cathedral. Besides, you look very angry with me, and I would rather not be with you right now. I've had enough of people being angry with me my whole life, I …" she puts her hand to her mouth. She's remembered again.

"Who's been angry with you your whole life, Merry Belle? What have you remembered?"

She looks at me, startled. "I don't know, Deus, it just seemed the right thing to say. It's what I feel inside. It's not a memory as such, just the feeling of disappointing people, but I don't know why. It's strange."

I stand in front of her and lift her chin with my finger. I kiss the tip of her nose. I love how her eyes go wide when I do this, and the colour creeps up her face and then she usually looks away. This time, she stares right back at me. I hold her cheeks with both of my hands. "I'm so sorry I looked angry. It is nothing to do with you, and everything to do with me. I'm not angry with you, Merry

Belle. I could never be angry with you. I'm also sorry you've had to be with angry people throughout your life. If I had my way, well …" I break the contact and turn my back on her. I don't know where this is coming from, but we need to leave, or she will be late. I feel her hand on my arm, and I turn to look at her over my shoulder. She's so small next to me.

"Deus, if you had your way, what?"

I let out a breath and run my hand over my face. "It doesn't matter. Come on, Merry Belle, you don't want to be late. Let's get you wrapped up. I can see the snow really coming down out of that window up there." I nod with my head. She gives me a small smile, and we head out to the cathedral, with me holding her hand. This has become the norm for me. I just need to be touching her.

I half wish she doesn't get her memory back because I know as soon as she does, she'll be gone.

I wish we could do this, be 'US' for a long time.

I wish she'd never come into my life because I know she's going to rip my heart out.

We head into the cathedral, and Monsignor Ruder is there to meet us. He shakes my hand in greeting and then takes Merry Belle's hand and bows slightly to her. She nods back at him, and she has an air of grace about the way she does this that I find a bit odd. "Deus, would you like to take a seat to listen to the choir? I will take Merrigan to where the choir will be situated and have her stand to the side so she is out of view as she requested." He smiles at her, and she smiles back.

"Yes, sure, I'll sit at the back so no one thinks I'm just trying to stay warm by being here."

He looks at me with pity on his face. "You can come and sit to the side where Merrigan will be if that makes it any easier for you, and Merrigan doesn't object."

She looks at me. "Yes, Deus, come be with me. I would love that and having you there will relax me and help my nerves."

I nod to them both, and Monsignor Ruder leads us both towards the altar and through the right side. The cathedral is empty at the moment. "Monsignor, why are there no people around at the moment?" Merry Belle asks him.

"On the run-up to Christmas, we close the cathedral to the public an hour before the choir is due to sing each evening. This is merely so we can get things set up. We have mass seven times a day, and we have guided tours throughout the day, so it's difficult for the choir to get set up during these times. They do practice in between mass and prayer times, but it's difficult for them. You were lucky you came in just at the right time today. It was meant to be, Merrigan." He looks up to the gold cross at the altar and marks the cross out on himself.

I look around. Even though I'm not religious, I'm in awe of this place. It's pristine, and I had no idea it was as big as it is inside. There is so much to look at with all the stained glass windows and the organ above the altar. We head to the side, and Monsignor Ruder shows me where to sit, next to Merry Belle. The choir are all in place and just warming up. He hands Merry Belle some pages, which I presume are the hymns she will be singing along to. "Now, Merrigan, if you don't want to sing any of them, that is fine, just leave them out. You can sing along to the ones you want to."

I can see she's nervous, so I hold her hand. She smiles at me, and I automatically lean in and kiss the tip of her nose. She pulls away and looks me in the eye, then looks at my lips, while licking her own. Shit. I could just lean in and kiss her. I want to just …

"Ahem, sorry to interrupt but we are about to start. The doors have been opened, and the cathedral is filling up nicely." Monsignor Ruder interrupts us, and we look straight at him like children caught being naughty. I look at Merry Belle, and she is blushing. The music starts, and she stands up in front of me with her back to me, pages in hand. She hasn't practised with the choir, but you would never know. She starts right on cue and the sound coming out of her mouth is just mesmerizing. I'm floored by it and sit still, just watching and listening.

Before we know it, the choir is leaving, and it's over. I could listen to her singing all night. She's amazing. She turns to me, and I stand up and take her into my arms. "Wow, Merry Belle, you were amazing. You have no idea just how good you are."

A lot of the choir members come to Merry Belle and say exactly that. They said she should be out front with them, but she tells them she is happy where she is.

We do this every day for just over a week. We come during the day, I help out where I'm needed, and we have food and drinks and a bed each night. The cathedral is getting busier and busier. I put it down to the fact it's Christmas in a few days, but Monsignor Ruder says that word is getting out about Merrigan and people are travelling from afar to come and hear her sing with the choir. To be honest, I can believe it. Last night, Merry Belle actually stood out with the choir to sing the very last hymn. They gave her a choir robe so she looked like part of the choir and not like a homeless person. She's attracting a lot of attention. She's still slowly remembering some facts about her life, but nothing of significance. I'm praying each day she doesn't remember. I know its wrong of me, but spending this time with her and getting to know her personality as she is now, well, she's perfect. I also know

I've fallen for her hard. After the awkward moment we had the first time she sang with the choir, we have only held hands like its natural. I kiss her on her nose, and we cuddle at night, pulling our beds together. I never want to let her go. It's just occurred to me. I haven't had one nightmare since having her in my arms. I can't let her go now.

CHAPTER ELEVEN

Merrigan

I CAN'T BELIEVE I ACTUALLY went out and stood with the choir last night. I let people see me sing. I still close my eyes when I sing, but when I opened them and saw how full the cathedral was, with everyone was standing up, applauding, I was shocked. I turned to Deus, who was at the side watching, and even he was applauding me. I gave him the biggest smile, which he returned. He melts my heart. I've been remembering little bits about my past, mainly names of people I must know, but I'm not able to picture them. I get frustrated because I thought I would have my memory back by now. The hospital said maybe in a few days, but that was over a week ago. I don't tell Deus everything I remember, not now anyway. I did at first, and I know he's happy when I tell him, but I also see the horror on his face each time he realises I've remembered something. I know he doesn't want me to leave. To be honest, I don't want to leave him. When I think about it, my heart hurts. I couldn't bear being without him now.

As we left the cathedral last night, I noticed a news van outside but didn't think anything of it. You see film and news vans all the time in New York.

As we arrive at the cathedral today, we stop at the Santa who is always outside on the pavement. We say a quick hello and make a Christmas wish. This has become a nightly ritual. We never tell each other our wishes, but mine is to not like the life I had before and to stay with Deus, no matter how we live. Although I worry about how that will be. It's all right for now because the Monsignor has given us a bed until after the holidays but what then?

As we walk, chat, and start for the cathedral steps, I notice even more news vans parked curbside. A few different stations are here, and I don't know if it's for something inside the cathedral or out on 5th Avenue. We head inside, and the place is full to the rafters. We only arrive ten minutes before the choir starts singing, as I don't need to be there any earlier, and I see TV cameras set up everywhere we look, and so many people.

We make our way through the throngs of people to the altar where the choir is almost ready to go. I rush to the side and put on my choir gown. I promised the Monsignor I would stand out with the choir for the duration and also do a solo. I don't mind. I just close my eyes and get lost in the lyrics and music. Suddenly, the entire place goes silent, and we start our first hymn.

My knees are shaking at the thought of singing a solo. However, I get the feeling I've done this before, even all the TV cameras around aren't bothering me, which is a bit strange. We get through the set, and it's time for my solo, I look at the side and see

Deus smiling at me, and he nods letting me know I've got this. I smile and nod back. I sing my song, closing my eyes and getting lost to the moment. When the last song is finished, the applause is deafening, and I stand in awe, smiling at the whole congregation, standing and applauding. I turn and head to the side and straight into Deus's arms. He kisses the top of my head and hugs me to him. "Merry Belle, that was perfection. You are a natural up there." He kisses my head again, and I look into his eyes, and we both stand smiling at each other. He leans down and gently kisses my lips. I melt into him.

I hear someone approach, and I turn to see Monsignor Ruder, standing there just waiting. "Oh, Monsignor that was wonderful, singing out there tonight with so many people. Does it always get like this at Christmas time?

He smiles at me and shakes his head, no. "No, Merrigan, We are always busy and yes, even more so leading up to Christmas, but this is so overwhelming to us all. This is all because of you. The TV crews and all these people are here for you. I hear all the whispers about the new lady singing in the choir, and I've had news stations phoning me asking who you are. I hope you don't mind, Merrigan. I told them you just appeared, but I didn't tell them your circumstances. That's not my story to tell."

I'm shocked that this is all for me. I thought this was normal with it being Christmas soon, and the cathedral being so popular. I don't know what to say.

"Merry Belle, I keep telling you that you have no idea how you sound. I'm not surprised this is for you, you deserve it."

I look at Deus, and I see the pride on his face, but I also see the sorrow in his eyes. His smile doesn't reach his eyes, and I know why. I turn to Monsignor Ruder. "Thank you for not telling anyone. I really appreciate that, and I also don't want to speak to anyone about it. I would rather not be on the TV, but I suppose it's too late for that now. Can we please use the back to leave tonight? I don't want to see them outside."

He nods then turns and leaves.

"But Merry Belle, this is your chance to be found. You can find out who you are," Deus says as he looks down. He can't look me in the eye because I will see the pain there. He knows he will lose me.

"I don't want all this attention, Deus. I don't want people knowing why I'm here, but I'm also scared that if this is televised, then someone who knows me will come and get me. Deus, I don't want that. I don't want to know the life I had before. I'm happy here with you. I feel this is the first time in my life I've been happy. I've had memories come back, and in them, I don't think I was a nice person, Deus. I think I may have been mean, and I'm scared to go back to that."

I turn to get my coat, and Deus spins me around to him. He crouches to look me in the eyes. "What do you mean? Why do you think you were not a nice person, Merry Belle? The person standing here in front of me is the nicest person I know. You are kind and compassionate, thinking of others when you have nothing. Thinking of me all the time, even though it's my job to protect and think of you. You could never have been a mean person, Merry Belle, never."

I look away. "I remember telling people what to do — like ordering them about. I remember shouting at some girls who I think were my friends. I was mean to them. I remember throwing my phone. I remember I did something bad, at least I feel I did something bad, but I'm not sure what it was, and I ran away from my parents. I think I was horrible, Deus."

He pulls me into his chest, and I wrap my arms around him, taking the comfort he's giving me. We just stand there for a while before he bends and kisses the top of my head. "I'm scared too, Merry Belle."

I look up at him. "Why, Deus?"

He lets out a breath and then looks down at my lips. He leans in and kisses me properly, and I respond. I have tingles running through my body from just the touch of his lips. I melt in his arms, and we forget where we are. We deepen the kiss — he's pressing into me and me to him. I can't get close enough to him. My heart is melting in my chest. We hear a cough and break apart. I drop my forehead on his chest, too afraid to turn around. I'm embarrassed.

"If you're ready to leave, I can show you the back entrance, as there are still TV vans on 5th Avenue. I suspect they are waiting for you to leave, Merrigan."

I turn to face Monsignor Ruder. I think my face must be bright red at the fact that a man of the cloth just caught me kissing someone in his cathedral. I feel so embarrassed. "Thank you, Monsignor. Yes, we are ready to leave." I look at Deus, who is looking down, smiling at me, and he nods. He takes my coat and puts it on me, along with my scarf, hat and gloves, then leans in and kisses the tip of my nose like he always does. He takes my hand, and we follow the Monsignor to the back exit.

"Merrigan, I understand if you do not wish to sing with the choir anymore — or at least until the excitement has died down. But then I fear the news channels will not leave this alone until they discover the person behind the voice. I am truly sorry you have to go through this." He looks really sorry, as though this is his fault.

"Please, Monsignor Ruder, none of this is your fault. I love singing with the choir. I feel this is my calling. Just being here in the cathedral feels like home, and I feel at peace when I am out there singing. I know you're right and the press will hunt me down no matter what, so I will continue to sing until Christmas is over. I don't want to let you down, and the one good thing coming from this is that your collections are increasing from all the visitors, which in turn is helping out a lot of people like Deus and I that are homeless. Even just doing it for that makes my heart melt. Thank you for everything you have done for us." He looks a little embarrassed but nods at us as we leave. Deus has me tucked into his side, and we go around the block, unseen by anyone.

We're not far from the shelter when I remember he didn't answer my question. "Deus, you didn't tell me why you were scared about me being found when I asked you earlier?" We stop, and he turns me to face him. The snow is coming down thick again, and I wipe at his eyelashes as the flakes stick to them. He leans down and kisses me again like he did in the cathedral.

"Merry Belle, it scares the shit out of me because I don't think I could bear to lose you. I know when you get your memory back, or someone comes for you, which I know won't be long now, that you will be gone, out of my life, and I can't stand the thought." He pulls me into his chest, and we stand there like that for a while, the snow sticking to us.

I pull away and look up at him. "Deus, it scares me too. I don't want to lose you. I don't know what my life was before, I think from the bits I'm remembering I was someone I don't like. I can't say who or why I think that but it's a feeling I have. If and when they come for me, I won't leave you, Deus. I've fallen for you, and it would break my heart. I will do everything in my power to be with you, one way or another." I stand on my tiptoes, and I kiss his cold lips. He doesn't kiss me back. Oh, what have I done? I shouldn't have said that. I pull away and look at him, trying to read his face.

He then rubs his gloved hand over his face and exhales. "Merry Belle, shit. I never wanted to be responsible for anyone again in my life. I never wanted anything like this, but I have never had feelings like this before for anyone. You've suddenly turned my world upside down. With you, all I want is to protect you, to cherish you, and to love you. I do love you, Merry Belle. I have, since I first saw you on the sidewalk, I couldn't leave you at the hospital. I was at war with myself, in turmoil, and I went against everything I'd ever decided so I could stay with you. I want you to be my responsibility. I want you, Merry Belle. I want you with all my heart. I want a life with you." He grabs both my cheeks and leans in to kiss me, pouring all his feelings into that kiss. I feel it everywhere. I feel all the love he has for me. I love him too. I pull away.

"I love you, Deus." Forehead to forehead, looking into each other's eyes, we smile at each other like two kids, all giddy. "Who knew, Deus? I feel this is the life I want with you. Well, maybe not the homeless and living off scraps part, but if that is how we need to live, then I want to be by your side, wherever that may be. I don't care."

"Me too, Merry Belle, me too."

It's late when we get back to the shelter, but we have our beds. This time, I get into his small bed with him, and we cuddle, kissing and touching each other, but nothing more. There are too many people around for that. We just explore each other as best we can with clothes on. I take his dog tags in my hands, running my hands over the inscription, but not being able to read it in the dark. I feel his abs. I never knew he was so ripped. It reminds me of the strippers who posted that video of me and why … Oh no, I remember. I remember that night, and why I shouted at my friends. I remember their names and where we were. I start to cry as the memories flood in.

"Hey, what's wrong, Merry Belle? You're freaking me out. Tell me what's wrong?" He has my face in his hands, and he leans in and kisses my tears away. I tell him what I remember, and where I was, which is why I have the tan. I remember I had security, and I escaped them to run away. I don't remember why I had security, or why I had to run away, but I'm sure it won't be long. He doesn't say anything. We both stay silent until we fall asleep, holding each other.

I wake up to an empty bed. I sit up in a panic. Where is he? He would never leave me alone. Even when one of us needs the bathroom, we wait at the door for each other. Why would he leave me? I remove the blanket that's covering me and sit on the edge of the bed to put my shoes on. I look around, and his backpack is gone. I start to panic. Would he leave me? Deus wouldn't do that, he loves me, and I love him? Was it too much? Did he think about it and realise he couldn't be responsible for anyone else — for me? He hasn't told me his story yet, and I haven't pressed him for it.

When did he leave? I didn't feel him get out of the bed. I must have been dead to the world in his arms for the first time since I was attacked. I can't believe he would just leave me. I feel the tears start to streak down my face, and I wipe them away, getting angry with myself when I don't know where he is? How could he do this? It's not that I can't look after myself: it's that I want him more than need him. We said we loved each other last night. My mind is racing, but I'm worried about him. I just didn't think Deus would ever do this. He said last night he couldn't bear to lose me, but he's gone.

CHAPTER TWELVE

Devs

I FREAKED OUT WHEN SHE FELL asleep in my arms. All I could picture was her beautiful face staring at me as I told her I loved her. I do love her, and I loved her falling asleep in my arms, but I lay awake for ages, unable to sleep, my mind going into overdrive. I started to freak about being responsible for her. What if I couldn't look after her and something happened? It would kill me if I lost her. I just thought it better to get out now, than wait to see how it all played out with her life.

It sounds like she's someone special, from what she's been saying about the Maldives and her security. I couldn't compete with anything like that. I couldn't give her the life she's known, and I'm sure as soon as all her memories come back, and she remembers who she is, she'll want to go straight back to that life and not live on the streets with me.

But then, we wouldn't have to live on the streets. I have a beautiful farmhouse that I bought years ago. It's in Austin, that's where some of my team were from. I boarded it all up and just left, but I know it's safe. I asked my cousin to keep an eye on it until I decided to return — if I returned. I also have a lot of money in the bank from my service in special ops, my retirement fund, and my compensation for being injured while on a tour of duty. I have a nice nest egg that's just growing and growing every month.

All this was going around in my head, and I couldn't do it. I felt myself starting to hyperventilate — the beginning of a panic attack, a major meltdown if I didn't get away and out of there quickly. I lifted her arms from me slowly, trying not to disturb her, lowering her head gently onto the pillow. She was flat out and didn't flinch. I stood up, and I felt like the floor was opening up to swallow me. I felt like I could just keel over at any second. The sweat was pouring off my brow and running down my face, but I was freezing to the touch. My vision was all wavy. It was like tunnel vision, and the walls were all moving in on me. I bent down, putting my hands on my knees for support before it enveloped me. I breathed in and out, over and over, taking deep, deep breaths until I felt somewhat normal.

Once I felt I could, I stood up straight and turned to look at her. Her beauty was mesmerising, and it calmed me down. It made me feel serene. I don't know how, but it was like taking my meds prior to becoming homeless, the ones I no longer take. I just stood there, calmly, watching her sleep for what felt like hours. I knew she would be safe enough in the shelter after spending nearly two weeks there. They all knew us, and they knew Merry Belle sang in the choir. She wouldn't have to go searching for food and only had to get to the cathedral and back. I would watch her from a distance to make sure she was safe getting there and back. I didn't care about me. Once she was back at the shelter from her singing, I would bunker down close by.

I left her a note. I got the paper and pen from the desk at the entrance to the shelter where I sat and wrote to her:

Merry Belle,

Please know I meant every word I said to you last night. I do love you. I love you so much that this is tearing my heart apart. I watched you sleep for hours. I found it so hard to tear myself away, but I had to do it. I had to leave. I will never forgive myself for leaving you, but I know you will be home where you belong very soon. Of that, I have no doubts. I also know you are safe here in the shelter until your family comes for you. I have a lot of demons that I've not told you about. I was starting to go into meltdown while you lay in my arms. The thought of being responsible for another person again gave me a panic attack. I have PTSD, Merry Belle, and it's not something I want you to witness. That would break my heart too. No matter what, I will always love you. You are a shining light and have helped me more than you could ever know. You show such compassion for others, and I know you love me. I felt it every time we touched. To kiss you was like you breathing new life into me. I wish it could be different, but you don't belong in this life, in my life. I knew when we met you were special and that this life is not for you. You will always be my princess, Merry Belle. I will never forget you, and I hope you find you have a loving family and someone special waiting for you back home.

My Christmas wish came true, Merry Belle. I love you so much.
All my love forever, Merrigan,
Your Amadeus (aka Deus)
Xx

Why do I do this shit to myself? I love her so much. I watch the shelter constantly, not wanting to take my eyes of it and miss her. I know she will go into a panic when she wakes up. It's still early, but she suddenly appears in the doorway, frantically looking around. She can't see me. I'm well hidden from view down an alley. She hasn't even put her coat, hat and gloves on. She'll freeze to death in this weather if she leaves without them. "Please, Merry Belle, go back in and get something to eat before you leave, and cover up. Please, for me," I start talking to myself. I feel someone pass me, which startles me because I'm too focused on her. It's a homeless guy, just going out to start his search for scraps. He looks at me as though I'm crazy. I probably look it, standing here talking to myself.

It tears at my heart watching her looking up and down the street for me. I can see the anguish and the pain on her face from here. I know at this moment she feels alone in the world, wondering where I've gone and why would I just leave. I can't let her see me having an attack. I go into meltdown. I don't want her to see me like that.

PTSD can be so debilitating. I've learnt over the years to control it on my own, but that's because I haven't had the responsibility of anyone. Taking on the responsibility of looking after Merry Belle permanently could set me right back if I let it.

Or she could help heal me? I haven't had one nightmare or flashback since she's been with me. Is that because I've been concentrating on protecting her? I don't know.

I watch as she hangs her head and turns back inside. I hope she finds the note I left in her glove. I thought that would be a safe place to leave it. I hope she understands. I still feel like the biggest shit in the world, but I think she will be better off without me. I just know her family will be here to pick her up soon, with all the news channels on the hunt to find out who the mystery lady with the voice of an angel is. Someone she knows is sure to see it.

I stay where I am and sit on the floor, waiting for her to come out. I hope she doesn't leave until she has to for the cathedral. The only time I have to move is to use the bathroom a little farther down the alleyway I am currently sitting in. I hope I didn't miss her. I get my watch out of my backpack to see what the time is. I never use my watch, but I need to know. It's coming up to 6.30 p.m. I haven't eaten anything all day. I will try to find something to eat once she is singing, and I'll listen from outside.

There she is. Thank god I didn't miss her. I sign the cross on my chest. I do that more since we've started going to the cathedral. I get up and follow at a safe distance. She's walking with her head down. I watch as she stops at the usual Santa Claus on the corner. She doesn't rush, but stands and stares at his pot. We have a ritual each day to make a Christmas wish. I wonder what her wish is today? She heads up the steps to the cathedral, avoiding eye contact with anyone. They would just think she was a normal tourist, covered up like she is with her scarf covering most of her face. The TV crews are all there outside, and I suspect inside, just waiting for her. I just realised today is the day before Christmas Eve. What a shitty thing to do to someone so near Christmas, break their heart. Could I feel any lower than I do right now? There are masses of people around. The clock strikes 7 p.m., and the choir starts to sing. I'm on the steps, listening. Normally, I wouldn't be able to hear much with the doors shut, but there are so many people here tonight, they're all crowding outside and down the steps and the doors are ajar. I'm mesmerised by her voice. I have tears in my eyes, which are freezing to my cheeks in the bitter cold. I can't help but think of her standing in there, sad, but still singing her heart out.

I hear a bit of commotion and turn to see a big black Cadillac with a police escort pull up outside the cathedral. This is a state car displaying flags of a country I don't recognise. As the car comes to a stop, a team of security immediately surrounds it before the doors are opened for the passengers to get out. I see a lady come out first, being helped by a man who must be her aid. She's very elegant, in a full-length coat that looks like it could be cashmere and a hat and gloves to match. I can't see her face clearly because her head is down as she is being helped up the steps to the cathedral, surrounded by men. There are three other passengers, all male. One is older and could be the lady's husband. He too is smartly dressed, again, in a full-length camel-coloured coat with leather gloves and a trilby hat. He has a dark complexion. There is a much younger man who could be their son. He has dirty-blond hair, and a dark complexion too. He is quite a good-looking young man from what I can see of his face. He's in a long coat, but his is one of those thick, skiwear coats with a hood full of fur. The third man, I don't like at all. He looks smarmy, as though he is above himself. He looks too old to be their son. He's in a long coat like the first man, only his is black, with black gloves, scarf and hat. He walks ahead of the younger man like he is more important. They all walk into the cathedral, surrounded by their security team, and armed police make their presence known on the steps. They are drawing a lot of attention to themselves, and I'm not sure if they are diplomats or royalty. The grace the lady had tells me she could be royalty. I watch as they disappear into the cathedral.

I move up the steps nearer to the doors to see if I can see what's going on. A police officer growls at me and nods his head, telling me to move away. I step to the side, where I can still hear the choir singing. As long as I can still hear Merry Belle, I don't really care who they are. Suddenly, Merry Belle stops singing midline, something's wrong. I move forward again. I want to get in and see that she's okay. I feel myself start to panic.

The officer who growled at me is watching me. "Sir, please move away," he growls at me.

I need to get in. I don't give a shit what he says. I start to move towards the door. He steps in front of me. "Sir, please move away, or I will be forced to remove you."

It's because I'm homeless. He thinks I'm going to make trouble. "Please officer, my girlfriend is in there, and I need to get to her. She just stopped singing. I know there is something wrong."

"Sir, I won't tell you again. Step away."

Shit. I need to get in.

I run down the steps and run around the block to the back exit of the cathedral, almost slipping a few times on the snow. The door is open, thankfully, so I head inside. The choir is still singing, but not Merry Belle. Something's wrong, I know it. I head to where I normally sit watching her, and I stop when I see her still standing out in front of the choir. She's just staring at the front row where the people I saw entering earlier are sitting. She must sense me because she turns to look at me. I see the anguish written all over her face, and tears streaming down her cheeks. She looks back at the lady, then back at me, before she turns and runs to me. I take her in my arms, thankful she's here with me. Why did I leave her this morning? "Hey, Merry Belle, look at me. I'm so sorry for leaving you. Please forgive me, baby, I love you so much. It broke my heart, but I realised I couldn't stay away. I've been with you all day, making sure you were safe." I crouch down to look her in the eye. "Do you forgive me, Merry Belle?"

She nods her head, yes, and I kiss her nose. The tears are

streaming down her face. "Baby, please don't cry. I'm so sorry. Please, Merry Belle."

She looks up at me, and I can see the sorrow in her eyes. I wipe away the tears with my thumbs and lean in to kiss her on the lips. "Deus, they're here for me. My family have come for me. You were right in your note. As soon as I saw them enter, I knew they were my parents. Everything came back to me. I know who I am, and what my name is, and what I am. But, Deus, I don't want that life. I don't want to go back with them." She cries harder putting her head into my chest. Shit, that *was* her family.

CHAPTER THIRTEEN

Merrigan

I SAW THEM WALKING INTO THE cathedral as though they owned it, and as soon as I laid eyes on my mother, I knew immediately who she was. How could I not? We looked so alike. I stopped singing as all my memories came rushing back to me like a tsunami — wave after wave of memories. I'd previously remembered the Maldives and the girls, but now, I remembered the video of me with those strippers. Oh, No. They've come to take me back, only to throw me away again. Wait, isn't it the day before Christmas Eve — my twenty-fifth birthday? I'm supposed to be getting married tomorrow to him: Prince Carsten, who is sitting there watching me, looking at me with distaste like I'm the one who's been cheating. Well, he can go to hell with the rest of them. I turned to the side, automatically looking for Deus — knowing he wasn't there, but when I saw him, I couldn't help myself. I ran to him and flung myself into his arms. He apologised, thinking my state was due to him. Well, some of it was, but mainly, I didn't want to go back to them, I didn't want that life. I do love my parents and my brother, but I never wanted the throne. I can't and will not marry Carsten.

In Deus's arms, I feel a bit calmer, but I'm angry he left me, even though he's come back for me.

"When you stopped singing, I knew there was something wrong, and I had to get in here to you. I take it that is your family? The press will be going crazy about all this now. Who are you, Merry Belle?"

I look up at him, as he wipes my tears away again. I have to tell him. "My name is Princess Merrigan Louise Thornton of Lyntona, heir to the throne. Lyntona is a small European island you may not have heard off. But it's home." I look down. I know he's going to want to leave now. "The king, queen, and my brother, the Prince of Lyntona are out there waiting to take me home, along with Carsten."

He lets me go and steps back from me. I look at him and see he's at war with himself. I can see the confusion on his face. He rubs his hand over his head, pulling at his hair. "You're a Princess? A real-life Princess. I was joking when I said you were probably a princess. Oh my God, Merry Bel… sorry, Princess Merrigan. What do I do now? Do I bow to you? Kneel to you? What?"

He's raising his voice, and I can see the panic on his face. I step up to him, but he steps back again. It kills me. I want to be in his arms. I want him. I love him.

"I'm still me, Deus, I'm still your Merry Belle. I'm still your prin …"

"Stop. Don't you dare say you're my princess? Your everyone's fucking princess, Merrigan."

Wow, that hurt. I step back. I don't know what to do. I turn and look out as the choir is still singing. I don't have long before my mother comes looking for me. "Deus let's leave. Let's get out of here right now through the back exit. No one will see us. We can run away and go anywhere we want. Come on, Deus. Come with me."

He just stares at me. I don't know what he's thinking, but he looks like he's in pain, and it kills me seeing him like this. I step up to him and grab his hands, not letting him step back from me again. "Deus, I want you. I want to be with you. I told you yesterday that no matter where that was, I wanted to be with you — even if it's living on the streets. I don't care as long as I'm with you. I love you, Deus."

I can see the clogs working overtime in his head. His expressions keep on changing from anger, to pain, to panic, to love. He shakes his head, no. "It won't work. They'll find us wherever we go. They have all the money and power they need to find you, take you back, and do away with me. I know what power is like, Merrigan. I know how rich people are. I was Special Ops for the US Government. I was sent on missions for rich people, to rescue them from militants, sent to hostile countries to rescue rich people who'd got themselves kidnapped. I saved so many lives, not just rich people, but you know what? Of all the people my team and I rescued, it was always the rich ones who just acted as though it was their right that we were risking our lives for them. We rarely got a thank you from the rich ones. Your family will come for you no matter what. You're a princess, for God's sake."

Wow, that's the most information I've had out of him. I knew he served from seeing his dog tags briefly last night, but it was dark, so I couldn't read them, but it also now explains the PTSD he has and his fierce desire never to be responsible for anyone. He led a team, and I know something bad happened to him and his team. I bet that's why he made himself homeless. He says it was his choice because he didn't want any responsibility. He's a soldier. I couldn't be more proud of him than I am right now.

"Deus, I don't care about them. I want them to renounce me as heir to the throne. I don't want to be queen. I want to be with you, Deus. Please, let's just leave."

I see him go rigid, and he pulls free of my hands.

"Merrigan, who is this? Why are you talking to some vagrant back here, and why haven't you been in contact with us?"

I stiffen at hearing his voice. I turn quickly and get right up into his space. He's taller than me, but not quite as tall as Deus. "What are you doing here, Carsten? Why are my parents here? Who I speak to is none of your business. Leave me alone and take my parents with you." I turn back to Deus.

"How dare you speak to me like that, Merrigan. I will not tolerate this from my soon-to-be wife and queen. You need to come with me immediately. Your mother sent me to get you and is waiting in the car for you."

I look past him and notice my parents and Archie have vacated their seats. "No, Carsten. I will not go with you. I will not be marrying you, and I renounce myself from the throne. Now go and tell my mother that."

The look on his face is priceless. I turn to Deus who has the same look. "Let's go, Deus." I grab his hand and grab my things, then head for the back exit.

"Merrigan, stop." I ignore him and carry on walking dragging a stunned Deus behind me. "Merrigan, I command you to stop this instant. As your betrothed and your future king, I command you to come with me this instant."

That's it. I turn on him. Who the hell does he think he is? "How dare you tell me what to do? You are not my betrothed, Carsten. Didn't you hear a word I just said? I. AM. NOT. MARRYING. YOU. You will not be my king, you cheating cad. Does mother know about your meal with Davina Smork? Or should I say your meal of Davina Smork? Get away from me, Carsten, this minute, before I make a scene in front of all those people and camera crews out there. Run to mummy, and tell her I will not be going back with her to marry you. I have a life here now with Deus."

I look back at Deus, who is watching this all play out. Carsten looks him over. "What do you mean you have a life with him? He's just a vagrant off the streets — a tramp, Merrigan. How can you have a life with him? You've been gone less than two weeks. You couldn't possibly know this guy?"

I'm looking into Deus's eyes. "It only takes a minute to fall in love, Carsten. When you know, you know, but you wouldn't know anything about that, apart from looking in the mirror. You only love yourself; you're so self-centred. Deus is my life." I smile at Deus, and he gives me a small smile and nod. He walks to me and takes my head in his hands. He leans down and kisses me full on the lips, right in front of Carsten. I hear Carsten gasp and move, and the next thing I know, he has my arm in a tight grip and is pulling me away from Deus.

I see the look of rage on Deus's face when he realises what just happened. Oh no, I don't want him to touch Carsten. He will be thrown into prison for a long time for laying a hand on a royal.

I break free from Carsten's grip, and I place my hands on Deus's chest. "No, Deus, It's okay." I stand on tiptoes to get to his ear. "He wants you to do this. If you touch a royal, your life will be over. Please don't do it. Let's get out of here."

I take his hand, and we start for the back exit again.

"Don't you dare leave, Merrigan. Your mother will be enraged if you do, and she will have no option but to renounce you." I ignore him and just smile up at Deus. He smiles back down at me then leans in and kisses my forehead. He takes my coat and puts it on me as we walk out.

"I'm sorry, Deus. If I had known, I would never have got you involved. I really don't want to go back, but I don't honestly know where I stand in all this. Let's get back to the shelter. I have no doubt my mother will find me somehow. She'll want me back for the wedding tomorrow, but that will never happen. For now, let's just get away."

We stop just before we step out of the door. "Merry Belle, it's almost impossible to forget that I just found out you're a real-life princess. How do I even get my head around that? You don't belong in a shelter or on the streets. Now you remember everything, how can you even think about sleeping in a shelter, and not in the royal suite at the Hotel Plaza?" I scowl at him. How can he think that of me? I've lived with him, homeless, for nearly two weeks. "Look. I'm sorry. I didn't mean it to come out that way. It's just hard to wrap my head around it."

"Just because I remember my past doesn't mean I'll forget how I've been living for the last two weeks. It makes no difference where I came from, Deus, or what luxury I'm used to. I want to be with you, wherever that may be."

What if he still doesn't want me? After all, he left me this morning. "Deus, do you still want to be with me? I know you came back for me, but did you decide you wanted to stay before you found out who I was for real, or were you going to just leave again?"

He takes hold of my face and bends so he can look me in the eyes. "Merry Belle, your highness." He smiles and winks at me, and I slap his arm. "I couldn't be without you. I couldn't leave. I was across the road from the shelter all day, just watching. Then I followed you to the cathedral to make sure you were safe. I had a war going on in my head. Leave you because I didn't want you to see me have a breakdown or to come back to you because I couldn't live without you."

I swoon. "What is your decision, Deus?" He leans down and kisses me hard on the mouth. He wraps me in his arms, pulling me into him. "Merry Belle, I need to be with you for as long as I can. With you next to me these last two weeks, I haven't had any flashbacks or nightmares. You're my saviour, and I love you so much. With you, I don't want to live on the streets any longer. With you, I want a life — for the first time I want to live a normal life. I have never wanted that since I lost five of my team. I walked them straight into an ambush, and I blame myself for their deaths. They were my family, Merry Belle, and it destroyed me that I got some of them killed and some of them injured, including myself."

I have tears running down my cheeks as I listen to him. This is the first time he's opened up to me. I hug him tight to me. "Deus, thank you for telling me this. Thank you for letting me in. I want to be there for you. I want to help you through this, help you realise it was not your fault. You had no control over an ambush." I kiss his cheek. "Come on, let's get out of here and back to the shelter. We can talk more there."

CHAPTER FOURTEEN

Devs

I TUCK HER INTO MY SIDE AS we leave the cathedral and head for the shelter. I can't explain how I'm feeling right now. I'm so confused, but at the same time, I'm elated to know she wants me. She's a real-life princess who will be queen one day, but she wants me and not the crown. How can that be? I try to imagine being in her position and living on the streets for a couple of weeks, then to find out you're a princess. How would I feel? Would I say screw living like this and head for the nearest royal suite or would I stay as I am? To be honest, I think I would do exactly what Merry Belle is doing. I would say to hell with material things. If I loved someone as much as I love her, I would want to be with her no matter what, where, or how. I squeeze her tighter into me. She really does love me. She could run to a posh hotel, but instead, she's by my side on our way to a shelter. I think I just fell for her even more. She looks up at me, and even though I can't see the lower half of her face, her eyes tell me she's smiling. The aqua sparkle in them floors me.

Just as we round the block onto 5ᵗʰ Avenue, we come to a complete stop. There are security men blocking our way. Shit. I bet her family has got security on every block watching for us.

"Giles, step aside," she says harshly to one of the security guys.

"Sorry, Your Highness, I can't do that on the orders of Her Majesty Queen Astrid." He speaks into his wrist to let the others know he has us here. I turn Merry Belle around and start to head back the way we came, but before I know it, the security are blocking us again. I turn back the other way, but there are more of them coming at us. Then the Cadillac appears at our side. The window rolls down, and the queen speaks, "Merrigan, get into the vehicle." She doesn't acknowledge me, and I don't say anything to her. I don't bow — why should I? She isn't my queen.

"No, mother, I am staying here in New York with Amadeus," she says, grabbing my arm with both of her hands. Her mother finally looks at me, and I see the shock when she finally registers me. I don't look like most homeless men. I'm clean, but my hair has seen better days. It's very curly and long when it's wet, but most days I have it tied up in a bun on top of my head, although I am unshaven at the moment because the razor I have is blunt. I have my backpack, but apart from that, for a homeless guy, I don't look too bad.

I see the distaste as she eyes me up and down when the penny drops that I'm a vagrant. She's judging me, and she has no right to do that. She doesn't know me. I stand up tall, letting her know she will not belittle me. "Merrigan, I will not ask you again. Get into the car before I am forced to ask Giles to put you in the car."

I see the look of horror on Merry Belle's face. "Hey, baby. We can just leave. They can't force you into a car. That would be classed as kidnapping in the USA."

Merry takes off her glove and strokes down my cheek. I pull the woolly scarf down that's covering most of her beautiful face, and I lean in and kiss her lips gently. I know what this is.

"Merrigan, get in the car now," her mother says with such authority and distaste that I turn and glare at a queen. She glares right back at me. Merry Belle takes my hand and moves me away from the car, but the security move with us. She holds her hand up to stop them and shakes her head, no to them. I look at her beautiful face. Taking it in, I know this is it for us. I look at the grey woolly hat covering her head and her one gloved hand, taking hold of that one as well.

"Deus, look at me? She is a queen. She has diplomatic immunity anywhere she goes. She can force me into the car, and nothing would be said about it. She could have me on the jet within the hour and on our way back to Lyntona, and nothing would be said or done about it. If I don't get in the car now and try to talk to her, she will force me in there. I know you want to protect me, but if you try to intervene, you will be arrested and thrown into prison, no matter what. I couldn't bear for that to happen. That would destroy both of us. No matter what, Deus, we will find a way to be together. I love you. Now, I'm going to get into the car. They will drive off, leaving you here. Please go to the shelter. Please stay around here so I can find you. I will come back, Deus. I promise you. I will come back." She grabs my face, pulling it down so she can kiss me. We kiss for what feels like ages, but it's not, it's only seconds. I pull her into me, and she wraps her arms around me, squeezing me tightly. Neither of us can bear to separate.

It's a deep voice that brings us back down to earth with a crash. "Merrigan, get in the car this instant. You've caused enough of a scene, and your mother has asked you nicely. I will take action if you do not move yourself right now." Her father's booming voice penetrates through us. She pulls away, and I see the tears streaming down her face.

I wipe them away with my thumbs. "We will see each other soon, Merry Belle. I love you, baby. Now go." She nods at me then turns and heads for the car. Just as she is about to get in, she runs back to me, flinging herself at me. I squeeze her to me and kiss her forehead, as I look to the car and see her father nod to Giles, the big security guy starts towards us.

"Merry Belle, please go, baby. I don't know if I will be able to control myself if he touches you."

She turns and sees Giles heading to us. She looks up and nods. "I love you, Deus, wait for me."

I watch as the car moves away from the curb, followed by the police escort and the security men. A crowd of spectators has formed, watching this play out. I hadn't noticed them before now. I hang my head, pull my scarf up over my face so just my eyes are showing, and pull my beanie lower. I turn away from the crowd and walk. I walk and walk, not looking where I am, not caring where I am. I should go back to the shelter so she can find me. How am I going to live without her by my side? Not being with her today nearly killed me.

On my bed, with hers empty next to me, I find it impossible to sleep. I keep thinking of Merry Belle. Why did I let her go? We should have walked away together. Why did she give up so easily? Was that her way out? Was that her letting me know this isn't the life for her? Is she too stuck up for all this shit? NO, she isn't. She loves me, and she wants to give up everything to be with me. What if I go and be with her in her country? I could do that if it's what she wants? She was prepared to give everything up for me, so why not me go to her? I could do that. I don't have anything keeping me here anyway. I need to find her. I need to tell her that is what I'm prepared to do. I will go and be with her if her parents will let me. Shit, how do I find her? What if she's right, and they've flown her back to her country? I don't even know where it is. I've never heard of it before. I need to go and see Monsignor Ruder or maybe Caspian would be better? Someone who could help me find her country and get a flight there. It's too late now, but I'll go and see Caspian in the morning and see if he can help me. I think he would be the best one to help me out.

I can't sleep. I just lay here all night waiting for the morning, but secretly hoping she will come back to me. That she somehow talked her parents into letting her come and find me. I know they will have taken her home. They wouldn't let her be with me, no matter what. But, I feel excited, regenerated like I suddenly have a life, like I have a purpose again. I'm going to be with her, even if finding a flight on Christmas Eve will be tough. I can't relax. I feel like I'm caged in, so I leave and head to Casper's. I search the dumpsters for some scraps before I put a cardboard box on the floor as it's covered in snow, and I sit there waiting. Staff have been arriving but not Casp. I get funny looks from them, and none of them wants to approach me.

Just then, Casp and his wife come round the corner, and I shoot up off the floor. "Hey, Deus, not seen you for a while. I was really worried about you. Are you okay?" Macen asks me. She's always so caring and so concerned.

"Yes, erm, we got a shelter. Merry Belle has been singing in the choir at St Patrick's, so they gave us beds in the shelter and food."

"Oh, how wonderful, Deus, I was only saying to Caspian we need to go to midnight mass tonight. Will Merry Belle be singing tonight?"

I look at them both, she's tucked into his side just like I do with Merry Belle and it dawns on me that the love I've seen between these two so many times is exactly what I have with Merry Belle. I look at the ground. "Hey, Deus, Is everything okay. You look a little forlorn there? Hey, Macen, how about going and getting a coffee for Deus, baby?"

"Yeah sure." She smiles and pats my arm as she passes me. I watch her enter the back of the restaurant.

"Have you had anything to eat yet, Deus? I can get Macen to rustle some scrambled eggs and toast if you would like?"

I smile at him. These two are the nicest people. "I could do with a little help if you wouldn't mind, Casp?"

He looks at me quizzically. "Tell you what. Come inside out of this freezing cold. I don't know how you do it. Ten minutes standing here, and I can't feel my toes. Let's go to my office, and I'll get you the eggs and toast, and you can tell me what you need. How does that sound?"

I beam at him and nod my head. We head inside to his office. "You won't believe what I'm going to tell you, Casp, but it's the honest truth, and I just need to see if you can help me out please."

I tell him who Merry Belle is and the situation that played out last night — all while eating the best scrambled eggs and toast I've had for a long time.

CHAPTER FIFTEEN

Merrigan

S HE JUST WOULDN'T LISTEN TO me. As soon as I got in the car, we headed straight to the airport. I tried to protest, unwilling to get out of the car, but I'm now on the jet, and my mother and father refuse to listen to me. I told Deus to wait for me, but what am I going to do now? The only person who's spoken to me is Archie. Bless him. I feel he had no choice but to come to New York, with my parents not trusting him to stay home alone without their supervision.

I've been sitting, talking with Archie, and to be honest, it's the longest conversation we've had. I told him everything that happened because he asked. No one else has even bothered to ask me if I'm okay or how I've been. They can see I'm not my usual polished self, but they haven't even bothered to ask me why I'm like this.

We are just coming in to land at Lyntona. Great. I'm thousands of miles away from Deus, and it's breaking my heart with each mile that passes. We all descend the steps of the jet. Peter, my head of security, is on the tarmac waiting for me. He's brought my car. I walk up to him sheepishly. He doesn't look at me at first. "Peter, I am so sorry if you got the wrath of my mother. I didn't want to get you into trouble. Do you forgive me?"

He looks at me, and the corners of his mouth turn up slightly, and he winks at me. "You're safe, and it's all good, Your Highness." I climb in and beckon to Archie to join me instead of getting into my parent's car. I can't believe Peter is still here. I was sure my mother would have had his arse fired.

As we arrive at the palace, I start to climb the stairs to head to my wing. "Merrigan, you have one hour to get yourself cleaned up, then you will join your father and me in his office. We have a lot to discuss."

Great, just what I need. On entering my quarters, I feel nothing. I look around, and everything is insignificant. The opulence of my quarters is too much. I hate it. I open my door and ask Cassandra, my handmaid, to come inside. "Cassandra, I want you to get some help, and I want you to remove all the ornaments, pictures, vases, in fact, everything from my quarters while I take a shower. She looks at me, puzzled. "Do you understand me, Cassandra? I want you to take everything out of here, now, please." I open my wardrobe and look at all the designer dresses, handbags, and shoes. They do nothing for me. I start to pull them all out. "I want these all removed as well." I pile them all onto the chaise lounge.

In the shower, I stand there, letting the warm water wash over me. I can't help thinking about Deus. Will he wait for me? How long will he wait? It strikes me it's Christmas Eve. I'm supposed to be getting married today. No way in hell is that happening. My poor Deus. I can't stop thinking of him, all alone again. I picture him sitting on the bed in the shelter, watching the door for me to come back to him. I stand and cry my eyes out, then sink to the floor, pull my knees up to my chest and wrap my arms around them. I stay like this for ages. I don't care that my mother gave me an hour. I will be as long as I want. There's a knock on the door. "Merrigan, are you in there, Merrigan?" My mother. I can't remember the last time she came to my quarters. "Merrigan, I'm coming in." With that, she comes marching into the bathroom. I look up through the glass of the shower room I'm sitting in, the water still pouring over me. I see the shock on her face. She comes over to the shower and fully clothed, she comes in with a towel, shuts off the water, and wraps the towel around me.

"Merrigan, you have no idea the trauma you have caused your father and me. We have been frantic, trying to find you. I know you find it hard to believe, but I'm your mother before I'm your queen, and you scared the living daylights out of me by disappearing. I haven't been able to sleep for two weeks. We've had every possible source searching for you, but apart from the withdrawal of money in the Maldives, then the flight to Atlanta, we had no trace." She helps me off the floor and gets my robe to put around me. She leads me to the sofas in my living room, and we sit. She actually holds my hands. I can't remember the last time she even touched me. I look into her face, and if it's possible, I see compassion there. She smiles at me. "I'm sorry, Merrigan. I'm sorry for losing it with you about the video. Jackie, Karen and the girls came and explained everything to me — about how you did not even want those men on the Island. They also told me about

Carsten and the things he's been doing. I brought him with us to New York because I wanted to see for myself the reaction you both had and what I saw in the cathedral told me it was not meant to be. I will not force you to marry a man like that. I know it's for the monarchy, but I do want you to marry for love. Just like I did with your father."

I can't believe what I'm hearing. "Why couldn't you tell me this in New York, mother? Why did you have to bring me home to tell me this? I have just left the love of my life behind, and I don't know if I will ever see him again?"

I hang my head, the tears streaming down my face. She lifts my chin so I look at her. "I was shocked when I saw you, Merrigan. I was so angry when I saw what you looked like and how you avoided us. I was so hurt by your reaction to us. I couldn't speak to you, and I needed to calm down. I've been going out of my mind with worry since you disappeared, and I find you in the arms of a vagrant. I couldn't believe what I was seeing, so I reacted how I always react — with a stiff upper lip. I am the queen, after all. I have to be seen to be in control and command the control of everyone around me, including my vagrant daughter. When your father told me to calm down in the car, well, I saw red and took it out on you. I am sorry for that."

I nod. I know she has to keep her royal persona in public. I get that because she's taught me to be the same, but deep down, we are human like everyone else, with the same feelings. "But, mother, you wouldn't let me explain anything to you. I want to tell you that Deus saved me, probably saved my life, from the attack, then I lost my memory and ..." she puts a finger on my lips as I start to ramble. "Archie has just told me everything, Merrigan. I am so sorry. I should have listened to you before we left New York. I owe

Amadeus an apology. He saved my precious girl, and then you both fell in love." She hangs her head. I have never seen my mother like this before.

"Mother, you demanded I come home from the Maldives. Were you going to renounce me from the throne?"

She looks at me and shakes her head. "No, my sweet girl. You will make the most amazing queen one day."

I'm shocked. I thought they were going to renounce me and kick me out of the palace. "But, mother, I don't know if I want to be queen. I love Deus, and I have to be married before I can be queen. I want to be with him, even if that means renouncing myself from the throne. Mother, I know you and father are disappointed in me, but I love him. I don't know how long I can go on without him. We've only been apart a few hours, and it's tearing my heart apart. I feel like I can't breathe properly because he isn't near me. I feel so hurt in here." I tap over my heart.

She pulls me into her and rocks me in her arms. I don't ever remember my mother being so emotional or touchy with me in my life. "My sweet girl. You have got it bad. If you feel you can't breathe and your life is over, then you know you have something special. I had that with your father. I never told you the story, but we were never meant to be married. Our parents wanted us married to other people. However, we fell in love and defied them. You are just like us, Merrigan. I can't blame you. Now, you need some rest. We will sort all this out, but let's just enjoy the holidays first. Your father and I have a lot of things to do and discuss. We have mass tonight in the cathedral, and we would love you to join us, Merrigan. It's our tradition, if you remember? You have a solo to sing if you feel up to it, but I won't pressure you."

"Thank you, mother. Can I see how I feel later on?" She nods, gets up and kisses me on the head, then leaves my quarters. I sit, thinking about everything. Thinking about Deus and what he's doing. I miss him so much. I hope we get to see each other again.

I wake up some time later, disorientated until I remember where I am and what happened. Did I dream all that with my mother? I don't think so. It's dark out, the curtains are still open, but I can see it's night-time. It's also snowing, and it reminds me of New York and Deus. The tears start to flow. I burrow deeper into my bed, letting it engulf me. It hurts so much thinking about him, all alone. I want to be with him. I'm going to speak to my parents and see if I can go back to New York to find him. If I can't be with him there, maybe I can bring him back here. But how can I be with him here? The rules are I must marry royalty. Stupid rules. I stay wrapped up in bed for a while longer, remembering everything that's happened in the last couple of weeks. I smile when I think of us searching for scraps in the dumpsters. If my parents had seen me doing that they would be mortified. I remember all the good things that have happened, how free I actually felt, the times searching for food and just sitting on some cardboard, peacefully, with Deus.

Thinking about it, I don't think it was being free from my parents and their rule, but being free with Deus. It was Deus that made me feel like that. I remember all the Christmas wishes we made together, with the Santa on the corner next to the cathedral. The wishes of how I wanted to be with him forever. The wishes of being, happy with him. There were so many wishes, and they all revolved around Deus. I remember I wanted to give money to help the children. I can do that now. I will get in touch with Monsignor Ruder, and he can help me with that. I also need to thank him for helping us the way he did.

I get ready. I put on my jeans and a sweatshirt, and I feel comfy. If my mother wants me to go to the cathedral with her, then she will have to accept me like this. I've changed. I don't need all the designer clothes. I'd rather use that money to help the homeless. We don't have a big homeless problem here, but I want to do something to help those that need it. And those with PTSD, to make sure they get the help and support they need. I feel refreshed and rejuvenated, even though I'm sad that Deus isn't with me.

I head down to the drawing room to see if anyone is around. I hear some commotion down the corridors, and I have no idea what is going on. I descend the vast staircase, and it's only now I just notice the Christmas tree is up. It's as beautiful as ever. It's so Christmassy everywhere. I didn't notice any of it when I arrived. I stand, taking it all in, and it saddens me because Deus isn't here to rejoice in it with me, but it also makes me feel warm because it's familiar to me. I hear many people pottering about, most of the noise coming from the kitchen but some from the drawing room. I head there to see what's going on. My father's in a bit of a tizzy when he sees me. "Hey, daddy, what's wrong? What's all the noise about?"

He doesn't answer me straight away. He's thinking — I know that face. "Erm, well, it's, erm just the staff getting everything ready. We're… erm… having people here after midnight mass. Your mother invited a lot of people, those that travelled for your nuptials. She thought it only right they stay here for their troubles."

I blush, sorry they have to go through all this. "I'm so sorry, daddy." He comes over to me and takes me into his arms. "Okay, what's going on? Who are you, and what have you done to my parents?" I say laughing at him. He looks puzzled. "It doesn't matter, daddy. It's a joke, It's just both you and mother have hugged me today, and I can't remember the last time either of you ever did that." I shrug and go to move away.

He doesn't let me go. "Merrigan, you have no idea how we felt thinking we had lost you for good, thinking something bad had happened to you. We didn't know where you were or even if you were alive. We missed you so much, Merry. We love you so much, and I'm sorry we have been awful parents to you, but we both love you with all our hearts." Wow, where did that come from?

"I have some business to take care of, as does your mother. She said she wasn't sure if you were joining us for mass tonight, and I take it from your attire you have decided not to?"

I look down at my clothes then back up at him. It's only now I see my father has aged. I don't know why I've never noticed before. Maybe like them, I've been too wrapped up in my life. "I am going to mass, daddy. It's our tradition that I sing at midnight mass. I don't want to break tradition. I'm comfy like this, and I will be wearing this. I've lived like this for the last two weeks, and I've felt normal. I know we are not normal, but I want to change that. I want people to see we are just like them. I don't want to parade around in designer clothes. I'd much rather donate my money to good causes like the homeless. I was one of them, daddy, and it's how I feel."

He nods at me and kisses the top of my head. "I am so proud of you, Merrigan. You will be a great queen someday soon."

I leave the room to go and see if I can find something to eat amongst all the chaos before I leave for midnight mass.

CHAPTER SIXTEEN

Merrigan

ALL THE KITCHEN STAFF WERE running around getting things prepared for our guests, but I managed to rustle up some soup and bread. Chef was having a bit of a meltdown by the looks of it, so I left him to it. I had some time before mass, so I asked Peter to take me to *Tiffany & Co.* in town, I needed to get some presents for everyone. I should have done it before I went to the Maldives, but my head wasn't in it with my now-cancelled wedding taking over Christmas. I bought all the girls some beautiful earrings, for my mother I got a *Tiffany & Co.* Schlumberger platinum and diamond bracelet, and I bought cufflinks for my father, Archie, and Peter. I wanted to get something special for Deus. I knew I might not see him again, but I wanted to get him a gift. I knew he wouldn't appreciate anything too elaborate, so I just got him a personalised leather wallet. I noticed he had a wallet when I saw him sort through his backpack one time. It was old and worn. I also did splash out a little on some platinum coffee-bean-shaped cufflinks, a reminder of us drinking coffee together sat on the streets. Who knows if he will ever get to wear them?

All my shopping is in the car apart from my presents to Deus. I just wanted them in my handbag, something close to me for him. I don't have anything else of his, so this will do. I can't stop thinking about him. I keep wondering what he's doing. I smile when I'm thinking about him, which is all the time, but then I also cry thinking about him and what we had for those short weeks. One way or another, as soon as tomorrow is finished, I will be on a plane to find him. I promised him I would come back for him. I am not breaking my promise now.

I'm at the back of the cathedral, just putting on my choir robe. I hear people talking and look out and see my mother, father, and Archie have all arrived and taken their seats at the front to the side of the aisle. They are the monarchy seats. No one else is allowed to sit there. I walk out with the choir, and we start the service. Walking out here, all my memories flood back of being in St Patricks. I look around to see if Deus is watching like he always did. I know it's futile, but I do it out of instinct. I'm sad, listening as the Monsignor goes through his sermon. We sing as a choir, then it's time for my solo. To be honest, it's the last thing I want to do, but then I look out at all the faces staring back at me, and I know I don't want to disappoint anyone. I look over to my mother and father, and I see the pride written all over their faces. Even Archie is smiling back at me — now that's weird. He's normally scowling at me. I smile back at them, and I wipe away the tears I feel trickling down my cheeks. I see mother's brow furrow slightly, and I give her the slightest of nods to let her know I'm okay. The organ starts the intro, and I stand up tall, close my eyes like I always do, take a deep breath, and sing my heart out. This is for you, Deus, I think to myself.

I finish my song and take another deep breath. The silence in here is deafening. Usually, the Monsignor starts speaking, but no one says a thing. I slowly open my eyes to look around, and I burst into tears. Standing at the bottom of the steps in front of me is Deus. I rub my eyes. How can he be here? Am I imagining it? I move my hands away from my face and watch as he climbs the few steps up to me with the biggest smile I've ever seen on his face. I fling myself into his arms just as he gets to the top step. It's a good job he's strong, or we would both have toppled back down the steps. I kiss his face all over and kiss his lips. He does the same to me. I'm in his arms, off the floor, and I'm a snotty mess with tears streaming down my face. "How are you here? I can't believe it, Deus? How?" He's smiling at me, I suddenly hear everyone clapping and some hollering going on, which, when I look out, I see it's all my girls whooping. I didn't even see them in here. I look at my parents, and they are on their feet. My mother is smiling, and I see her wipe at a tear on her cheek. She grabs my father's hand and squeezes it, and he places his other hand over hers. She nods at me. I turn back to Deus and kiss him full on the mouth. I don't care that the whole congregation is watching me. He's here with me, and I'm in his arms.

"Baby, I missed you so much," he says into my ear as he hugs me to him.

"How are you here, Deus? How did you get here so quickly? Look at you. You look so handsome. I can't believe you're here." He twirls me around. Everyone is still on their feet, clapping. This is so unreal. He slides me down his body gently so my feet are on the floor, and he takes both my hands in his. "I will tell you everything later. Everything's happened so fast." He takes my face in his hands and kisses the tip of my nose. "I love you so much, Merry Belle, It physically hurts in here." He taps over his heart. I'm not sure I've stopped smiling or crying happy tears yet. He wipes my cheeks with his thumbs.

He pulls me into his chest, and we just stand there squeezing each other. I feel if I let go, then it will all just be in my head, my imagination running away with me. He breaks away, and it's then I notice he's in new clothes. Still, jeans and a white t-shirt but his dog tags are outside for all to see this time, which is a good sign. That tells me he's proud to have served. He's also in a leather jacket. He puts his hand in the inside pocket of the jacket, and as he's doing this, he gets down on one knee in front of me. He pulls out a *Tiffany & Co.* box and opens it. I gasp out loud, putting my hands to my mouth. Inside the box is a beautiful, but simple, solitaire diamond ring. He looks up at me, and I see tears in his eyes. "Merr…" He chokes up a little, stops to compose himself, takes a deep breath, then starts again. "Merry Belle. I know it's only been a short time, but it feels right. I was going out of my mind without you, and that told me everything. I can't be without you in my life. You are my princess. I love you more than life. I want to be with you forever. I want to love you forever. I want to protect you forever, and I want to have babies and grow old with you. Please, will you do me the honour of becoming my wife? Of becoming Mrs Stollinka? Of becoming my queen?"

I fall to the floor with him and fling myself at him, knocking us both backwards onto the floor. I'm now on top of him, looking into his face. "Yes, Deus, YES, YES, YES," I shout for everyone to hear. I know this is highly inappropriate, but at this moment I really don't care. I kiss him hard. I feel his tears running down his cheeks into my hands that are holding the side of his head.

"Erm, Merry Belle?" I look at him, still smiling. He turns his head to look at the congregation. I follow his gaze, realise everyone is still watching us, and blush. He looks at me and laughs. "I think we better get up and act appropriately while we are in here, don't you agree?"

I nod, laughing, and we both get up off the floor. He places the ring on my finger just as my parents join us at the altar. The whole congregation is clapping and cheering.

I cling to Deus, but internally I'm worrying. I can't marry him. He isn't royalty. My parents won't allow this. Oh no. What have I done? I look at my parents in horror, but they are both smiling at us. I furrow my brow.

"It's okay, Merrigan, we will explain everything to you," my father says as he leans in and kisses me on the cheek, before shaking Deus's hand.

My mother kisses me on the cheek. "Don't worry. I can see those clogs working. It's all fine, and you do have permission to marry Amadeus."

I breathe out and smile at her. She then leans in to kiss Deus on the cheek, and he bows to her. "Congratulations to you both. I couldn't be happier. I can see how much you love each other, and that means more to me than anything," she says to us both.

I throw myself into her arms and hug her to me tightly. "Thank you, Mum. Thank you so much. I love you." I kiss her cheek.

"One more thing, Merrigan. Now, this is entirely up to you because Amadeus does know about this. He has the option because we had a very long chat this evening about everything."

I look at her and my father. "That was the business you said you had to sort out?" He nods at me and smiles. I look back at my mother. "What is it, Mum?"

"Well, as most of the guests have already arrived for your wedding today and everything is still in place, we wondered if it was too soon for you to both get married now? You don't have to. You can have a long engagement if you both want, but it's plain to see to anyone you two are madly in love."

I'm shocked. I look at Deus, who is smiling at me. He winks, and I melt. "What do you think, Deus? Is it too soon? I know it's only been a couple of weeks, but I love you. That won't change. If you want to wait, then I understand completely. Fitting into my lifestyle will take a lot of getting used to. If y…"

He leans in and kisses me to stop my babbling. "Merry Belle, I don't care when we get married, all I know is, we will get married — the sooner the better as far as I'm concerned. But if you want to wait, then I'm happy with that too, but it won't be too long of an engagement. I don't want you to turn around and say we rushed this. You have a kingdom to think about as well. It's not just you and I in this. I love you, no matter what."

I kiss him. "Yes, I want this more than anything. Let's do it. I'm not losing you ever."

EPILOGUE

Dens

MY LIFE HAS TAKEN A TOTAL U-turn. I never wanted responsibility ever again, yet now I have more responsibility than I could ever have imagined.

The day Merry Belle was taken from me, I went to see Caspian, and I told him everything that had happened. It turned out he had actually been to Lyntona while filming his cooking programme. They had a speciality dish that he went to learn and put it on his 'Cooking Round the World with Caspian' show, and he had met the king and queen. It all fell into place for him; he said he thought he recognised Merry Belle from somewhere that first time he saw her but wasn't sure from where. Casp got in touch with the king's press office, and the king phoned him back from the plane, knowing it was to do with me. He wanted to speak to me. I was a bit apprehensive but took the call. I remember his first words to me: "One question, do you love my daughter?" I didn't hesitate. I told him that I did with all my heart. Seems that was good enough for him. He told me they were on the way back home and he arranged for a private plane to be waiting for me at the airport.

I landed only a couple of hours after they landed. He had Peter, Merry Belle's head of security, meet me at the airport, and he took me to the palace. Luckily, the palace was so vast, that as Merry Belle was in her own quarters, she wouldn't know I was here. I wanted to see her, not hide from her. He told me I had to see the king and queen before anything. Well, that was an experience. I was dreading it because I didn't want to disrespect them, but they made me feel so welcome. I was in shock. After sitting with them and being quizzed, they showed me to a guest suite so I could freshen up. While I was in the shower someone had entered my room and laid out lots of new clothes for me which included designer suits, jeans, sweats, t-shirts, all in my size. All I wanted the whole time was to find Merry Belle. I wanted to be with her, but they asked me not to seek her out — to be patient.

I then joined them for dinner in their private quarters so Merry Belle didn't see me. That was a very interesting dinner. They had me sign an NDA, which I had no objections to. I would never tell anyone anything private about the family. Then they told me that they had done checks on me, they knew all about my career, that I was highly decorated with a Distinguished service medal and a Silver Star, they commended me on my service, but the most interesting fact was, they found out about my ancestry, which in all honesty I had never looked into. It turns out that my family came from a very influential diplomatic background in Austria, and that my father was a diplomat of Austria. I had no idea. As I was from a diplomatic background, they had an amendment made to their rules of the kingdom, that a prince or princess may enter into matrimony with royalty or anyone from a diplomatic background. I couldn't believe what I was hearing. They asked what my intentions were, and I told them I loved Merry Belle (I had to explain why I called her Merry Belle, but they thought it was sweet), and that I suffered from PTSD and they vowed to help me with that. I told them I wanted to marry her because I couldn't live without her. They asked if I would have any objections signing a prenup agreement, and I told them none at all, as long as I was with Merry Belle, I would sign my life away. That seemed to be good enough for them. They explained all about their reaction and then about the planned wedding. We got married that night.

I am now King of Lyntona, and I proudly sit next to my queen. We have three beautiful children: Amadeus, who is now seven and is the image of me. Amber, who is five and is the image of Merry Belle, and then there is little Tamara who is almost three. She is an angel and is a mix of Merry Belle and me. I couldn't be more proud of my queen and my family. The responsibility is what I thrive on, and it's what I missed — I just didn't know it. We no longer have a homeless situation at all on Lyntona, and several other countries have followed in our footsteps. It was one of the most important things Merry Belle and I set about doing just after we got married. We also set up various help facilities for anyone suffering from any kind of PTSD.

It's Christmas Eve, and our 10th wedding anniversary. I always like to do something special for Merry Belle, just the two of us, before we all head to midnight mass where she still sings. We are having dinner together in our suite, and I have the most beautiful gift for her. I give her a Tiffany box holding a beautiful platinum eternity ring encrusted with diamonds and sapphires.

"Oh, Deus. I love it. Thank you so much. It's beautiful. I have a gift for you, now, close your eyes." I do as I'm told. She gets up, comes round the table to me, and puts something into my hand. I open my eyes to see another Tiffany box. I open the box and inside is a scan picture. I know exactly what it is. We've had three children, and it looks like number four is on the way. I pull her onto my knee. She squeals and laughs, and I kiss her. "Thank you, Mrs Stollinka. You make me the happiest man alive. Number four, hey, are we aiming for a football team?"

She laughs at me. "Actually, Deus, make this number four and five, see." She points to the two blobs on the scan.

"Twins?" She nods, yes, with a big grin on her face. "Tiffany and Sapphire, what do you think?"

Wow, and my family just keeps growing and growing.

"I love you so much. You and the children complete me. Thank you, Merry Belle. You are my hero. You saved me."

The End

REVIEWS

I really hope that you enjoyed this story. Reviews are lovely! Honestly, they are! And they also help other people to make an informed decision before buying this book.

I would really appreciate it if you took a few seconds to do just that.

Thank you!

Amazon
Goodreads
Bookbub
Lynda Throsby Xx

ALSO BY LYNDA THROSBY

Catfish

A dark, gritty, romantic thriller (this book contains graphic scenes) for 18+ only

The Best Day Of My Life

A sweet, single dad of twins romance

Chef

A semi dark romantic thriller

MORE ABOUT LYNDA

Lynda lives in Cheshire in the UK with her husband Peter and cat Bailey also with two grown-up daughters and has a 12-year-old granddaughter and a 10-week-old granddaughter

She runs a successful financial business with her husband.

As a young teenager, Lynda used to read horror books with a love for everything Stephen King and James Herbert. She has always wanted to write and even wrote horror stories at age 13.

A little later she started reading Jackie Collins and Jilly Cooper and has always had a love of books. This then exploded with Twilight and Fifty Shades of Grey. Oh, and the introduction of e-readers.

In her spare time, she has a season ticket for Manchester City Football Club and goes to all the home games. She loves going to concerts and the theatre. She goes to the cinema at least once a week. When the weather is nice you can see her gliding down the road on her Harley Davidson 1200T motorbike. Travelling is also high on the agenda, and her dream is to visit every state in the USA.

ACKNOWLEDGEMENTS

I wouldn't have done this without the help and support I got from friends and family.

First to my husband, who made time for me to write by running our business and the continued support he gives me, encouraging me to carry on.

Stuart Reardon again for being on my cover and to him and Peter for the cover picture.

Georgia Conlan my beautiful talented goddaughter for being on my cover. You are a star.

My family and friends who read the books and give me feedback.

My editor Claire Allmendinger for guiding me through and being patient with me, as always.

Sybil Wilson from Pop Kitty for the amazing cover.

Cassy Roop from Pink Ink Designs for the fantastic formatting and making my words look pretty.

Thank you to everyone who supports me and reads my words.

Lightning Source UK Ltd.
Milton Keynes UK
UKHW011528011219
354565UK00007B/168/P